D1510615

Destiny & TRENT

A Hood Love Story

A NOVEL BY

CANDY M

CHAPTER ONE

Destiny

"Drive, you piece-of-shit car!" Well that part wasn't true. I drove a BMW, so technically, it wasn't a piece-of-shit car. But right about now, it was getting on my nerves, and I was about to be late for school. Well, technically, I didn't attend school. I taught it. Pre-school that was—a bunch of runny nose, whining kids, but I loved them.

I had no idea what the problem with my car could be. My boyfriend, Miguel, bought it for me a few months ago, so there was absolutely no reason it should be acting up right now.

Groaning loudly in frustration, I grabbed my phone out of my purse as I pulled alongside of the road. I dialed Miguel's number and waited patiently for him to answer.

"Hey, baby," he answered after just two rings. I smiled. hearing his deep Keith Sweat voice.

"Miguel, baby, my car is acting up. It's behaving as if it wants to cut off on me," I whined like the princess I was.

"That shouldn't be happening. Just drive to the nearest mechanic shop, and later in the week, I'll take it back to the dealership."

I grunted. Like really, where was I going to find a mechanic shop?

"Miguel, can't you just come and get me?" I pleaded because the last thing I wanted to do was drive around, trying to find an auto shop.

"Baby, you know I can't do that. Go to Google Maps or something to help you find the nearest auto shop. Look, I gotta go. My client just walked in my office. Love you. Call me and tell me how everything goes." Without giving me a chance to protest, he hung the phone up.

"Ugh." I began biting the inside of my cheek in frustration. Making one last call to the private school where I taught, I let them know I was going to be late. Using Google Maps as Miguel said, I saw there was an auto shop about three blocks down, and I started driving in the direction of Turner Auto World.

Thank goodness they didn't have many cars. I saw just one parked in the garage as I drove my car in. Climbing out, I quickly smoothed out my black pantsuit that hugged my body. My body structure was very curvy, so no matter what I wore, every curve of my body was very much visible.

I looked around, and there was no one in plain sight. Pushing my glasses up the bridge of my nose, I walked to where the only car was parked and almost tripped over a pair of feet.

"Shit, I'm sorry. I didn't see you under there." I looked down at the pair of legs sticking out from under the car. He was clad in a dark-blue jumpsuit with a pair of dirty, black work boots on his feet. I only got a view from the waist down, but from what I saw, he had a nice, solid, toned body. What caught my attention even more was that bulge that couldn't possibly be his.

I shook my head because my thoughts were straying.

"Excuse me, can you help me, please? My BMW is acting up." I stood for a full minute, and I got no response. Tapping my three-inch heels with impatience, I cleared my throat loudly.

"Excuse me!" I yelled and rudely kicked the device he was laying on.

"Lady, you gon' have to wait your turn." His muffled reply only made me even more upset. Refusing to be ignored, I kicked the shit out of his ankle.

That definitely got his attention. Rolling from under the car, I took a step back at his sudden movement as he got up from off the ground, towering over my barely five-feet frame.

"Are you fucking crazy? Did you just kick my ankle?" His eyebrows were knitted together as he glared at me. But we were glaring at each other for two different reasons. He thought I was obviously some maniac, and I was gawking at him, not because he was rude as hell but because he was fine as hell.

His jumpsuit wasn't pulled all the way up, so only his lower half was covered. The other half was in full view, and his Butterscotch complexion was covered with tattoos. Both his arms had full tattooed sleeves, and his chest was covered with all sorts of pictures and writings. His face had a full, well-maintained beard, which surrounded a full set of dark-pink lips. His nose had piercings on either side, and his hair was styled in a high fade with the sides tapered down.

"Aye!" he said as he snapped his fingers in front of my face. Forget the fact that he was fine; this nigga needed to learn some manners.

"Do you call this proper customer service? You're rude as hell. Where is your supervisor? I would like to file a complaint."

Snorting at me, he reached for the sleeve of his jumpsuit, pushing his arms through and zipping it up. With his index finger, he tapped on the pocket of his jumpsuit... Trent Bishop: Supervisor.

Shit! He was the supervisor.

"You can go ahead and file your complaint to me," he said in a dry tone. Rolling my eyes at him, I folded my arms against my C-cup breasts.

"Trent, can you please see what's wrong with my vehicle so I can get to work." I raised my eyebrow suggestively as he licked his lips in a LL Cool J type of way. Eyeing me slowly from head to toe, he stopped when he reached the small scar on my forehead as if curious.

"What's wrong with it?" He started making his way over to where my car was parked, and I followed behind him.

"I do believe that's your job to figure out what's wrong with it, *Trent*." I stressed his name just to be a bitch. He gave me a hard glare as he opened the door and climbed in. The keys were still in the ignition, so he started the engine.

I spent thirty minutes in that garage until Trent finally had the problem fixed. Replacing the hood of my car and shutting it down tightly, he turned to me as I stood a distance away, allowing him to work.

"It took you long enough. How much do I owe you?" I walked briskly over to my car to retrieve my handbag so I could pay him and be on my way. I was so late for class that I wouldn't be surprised if they fired my ass.

"It's on the house, not because I appreciate your service but because I think it's time you left. You rude as fuck, lady."

I was standing there, trying to pick my jaw up off the floor because I knew he didn't just say I was rude.

"Me! You have some nerve. How'd you even get the position as supervisor? Did you screw your boss?" I asked as I smirked at him.

"My boss is a seventy-year-old white man," he explained as he looked me up and down as if he thought I was crazy.

"And?" I blinked my eyes at him because I didn't see the problem.

"Lady, I'm about to go back under that Ford and finish the job I started. Please, do not hesitate to find another auto shop if anything else goes wrong with your vehicle." His rude ass turned around and walked away from me. Sucking my teeth in annoyance, I was all too happy to leave as I jumped in my BMW and made my way to work, thankful that Trent and I would never cross paths again.

*****

"It's Friday, Destiny. What you getting into tonight?"

I took a bite of my cheese sandwich as I shrugged my shoulders at my friend and coworker Jamika. Let me say this before we move any further. Jamika and I had a good job that paid well, but we had our hood side to us. Don't get shit twisted.

We sat in the teacher's lounge on our lunch break, trying to eat as fast as we could because on Fridays, we were allowed to dismiss our students as soon as our lunch period was over.

5

"You going out with Miguel, or na?"

I instantly got annoyed at the sound of my boyfriend's name. We were supposed to go have a romantic dinner out tonight; instead, he canceled on me, saying he had to work late to prepare for a case on Monday. Miguel was a divorce lawyer, and his job took a lot of his free time. And to be quite honest, I was beginning to get sick of it.

"Nope, we not doing anything. I'm just gonna sit at home in my pajamas, eating my favorite ice-cream and watching some movies." Goodness, my life sucked.

"Ugh, Destiny, you lame as fuck." Jamika let the curse word pass her lips, knowing damn well she shouldn't be cussing. Last time she did, one of the kids heard and told on her ass.

"Jamika, stop cussing," I fussed at her, and she rolled her eyes at me.

"Since you're not doing anything, me and Julissa going over to Stallion City. I'm about to take you with me." I stopped midbite into my sandwich to gawk at Jamika because clearly, she'd lost her mind.

"Um, one, I hate Julissa… Ew! And two, Stallion City is a strip club. I'm not about to roll up in there." Jamika was a nutcase if she thought I would be seen in some sleazy strip club.

"Um, one, I don't know why you hate her so much, and two, you don't got shit else to do. So I'm picking your ass up at ten. I heard they got a new dancer named 'Dingo. It's alleged his dick touches his knee!"

I laughed at Jamika because really? His knee?

"Jamika, if you pull up in front of my house, I promise you I'm not coming out."

She laughed at me, and I knew my friend well enough to know that she was most definitely going to be parked in front of my house at the exact time she said she would be.

Sighing softly, I knew my Friday night was about to be spent inside of a strip club.

CHAPTER TWO

Trent

"Aahh! Trent, fuck this pussy, baby!"

I looked down and enjoyed the way my ten-and-a-half-inch monster was going in and out of LaLa's wet pussy. LaLa was one of the waitresses that worked in the club I danced at, and every now and then when I wanted a quick release, I would fuck her.

LaLa's pussy got wet as fuck, but her shit wasn't the tightest. And for having dick the size that I had, it should take a while to get all ten plus inches inside, but the first time I fucked this bitch, my shit slid right into home base. It had a nigga thinking she was fucking with horses or some shit.

"You love this big motherfucker?" I asked as I watched the way her ass slapped my thigh. Ass up, face down was how I liked my women, which was the exact position LaLa was in as I held on to a fistful of her hair. We were in the locker room in the club that I worked, and when I say we, I mean LaLa and I weren't the only people in the room.

"Yesss, baby... Mmmm." LaLa groaned in pleasure as I continued drilling her.

Smiling, I looked in the corner to where Tracey stood, casually smoking her cigarette, naked as the day she was born. Her eyes filled with lust as she watched the damage I was doing to her girlfriend. I nodded my head at her, which was the signal for me giving her permission to join LaLa and me.

Tossing the cigarette to the ground, she walked over to us.

"Assume the position, ma," I said to Tracey as I slowed my strokes down, allowing Tracey to get on her knees. LaLa and I were standing. One of her feet was on the small wooden bench to the center of the room, and the other was planted firmly on the floor. Her hand lay flat on the locker in front of her.

I looked down, enjoying the vision of Tracey sucking and pulling with LaLa's juicy clit.

"Ugghhh, fuck!" LaLa moaned loudly as Tracey made loud sucking noises against her pussy lips. Tracey and I made eye contact, and I winked at her. Unknown to LaLa, Tracey and I had been fucking behind her back, which was not part of the agreement I had when LaLa came up with the idea to invite me into their bedroom, only if I swore to only have sex with her girlfriend when she was present. But Tracey's shit was tighter than hers, so fuck an agreement.

Thirty minutes after my threesome, after having showered and dressed in my costume, I was getting ready to make my way to the stage. I stood behind the curtain, taking a look at the audience. I saw the usual thirsty females seated at the front of the stage—the ones who always wanted to touch my dick to see if it was real. I spotted LaLa working the floor, serving up alcohol to the patrons. Tracey, her girlfriend, was seated at the bar. I really needed to cool it with those two. Something told me when LaLa found out we'd been fucking behind her back all this time, she wouldn't be too happy on account that LaLa's ass was a little bit crazy.

My eyes fell on a table that had three women. I recognized one but not the other two. As I was about to look away, I focused my eyes on the one that sat in the middle. *Wasn't that homegirl from earlier in the auto shop?*

I squinted my eyes, making sure that it really was her. And I smiled wickedly to myself because guess who was about to get their very own private show. As the host of the club announced my intro, I adjusted my loin cloth as the jungle/African type music played in the background.

"And now coming to the stage, ladies, put your hands together for… 'Dingooooo!'"

I made my way onto the stage, and the women screamed, and the ones seated to the front got up and rushed to the edge of the stage, waving their money.

Standing directly in the middle of the stage, smiling, I eyed the women waving their bills at me. Using my hand, I trailed it along my naked, tattooed chest, slowly making it down my tight six pack. Upon reaching the loin cloth, I outlined the image of my monster, looking into the crowd for the person I wanted to see.

I smiled inwardly as our eyes connected. I wished I could take a picture of her face as she gawked at me, her eyes wide in shock. She had her lil' nerdy glasses on that made her look gorgeous in my book. She looked at her chocolate friend on her left and said something to her in her ear; something told me she was talking about me.

I decided that I should just go ahead and find out for myself. Making my way down the couple of stairs, the thirst traps scratched and pulled at me, trying to get their hands under my cloth to touch what they knew they couldn't handle.

With a big smile on my lips, I danced slowly, gyrating my hips as I walked to my intended target, who was now looking around her shoulder as if she was doubting that I was really bold enough to come to her.

Ignoring the women that screamed my name, I now stood in front of the table where all their eyes were glued on me in awe. My lil' rude, obnoxious friend that had so much lip earlier this morning in the auto shop was sitting there, speechless as fuck.

As I stood before her, wondering exactly how I should execute my revenge for her smart ass mouth, I rubbed my beard thoughtfully. She began to slowly shake her head, letting me know whatever I was thinking, I should just forget it.

My smile widened at her reluctance, and I made my way over to her as her friends screamed.

"Oh my God, Destiny!" her chocolate friend said as she slapped her friends upper arm enthusiastically.

I said her name over and over in my mind. The name suited her. She looked like a Destiny. I remembered her from earlier. She was short as hell and looked like she was barely over five feet. Her complexion was a nice light-brown color, and her hair was in its natural state, which actually stopped at her shoulders with a nice kinky curl. She had body for days; her curves couldn't be contained even if she tried to hide them, and she definitely had junk in the trunk.

Removing my hand from my beard, I looked her dead in her eyes and pointed my finger at her. Her head movement was now even more rapid as if she wanted to shake that shit off her shoulders.

Cheesing like crazy as I caressed my dick, holding her gaze, I did my signature lip lick and blew her a kiss as I walked to her.

The music in the background changed to Ginuwine's "Pony."

Way to go, DJ, I thought to myself as I straddled her lap, and her friends began screaming even more.

"So..." I said as I placed my lips against her ear. "We meet again, Destiny."

"Trent, get the fuck off my lap... Now!" she threatened me through clenched teeth. Finding her words humorous, I chuckled as I placed both hands to the back of her chair, making her my unwanted prisoner as I gyrated against her lap.

"Let's not spoil the show. Sit back and enjoy. Oh, and my name is 'Dingo; don't you feel him?" I thrust my hips into her lap so she could feel that she actually was making my dick hard, something that usually didn't happen during my performance, especially seeing how I fucked just before I got on stage.

Putting my hand on her knees, I eased her legs apart slowly, never taking my eyes off her. Continuing my gyrations on her lap, I began easing my way downward between her open thighs. The females in the audience were hollering like hell as I positioned myself between

Destiny's legs. With my face now planted right in front of her pussy, I looked up at her before closing my eyes, burying my face between her legs as I sniffed her. Her natural scent let me know that she was somewhat aroused.

Opening my eyes again, I looked up at her and stuck my tongue out and began stimulating movements as if I were eating her pussy.

"*Yass,* 'Dingo!" a few of the women from the crowd screamed. Deciding I needed to stop fucking around with Destiny's ass because my dick was now hard as fuck, I stood from my position. Taking her hand, I placed it on my chest, and all the while, she was trying to pull it out of my reach, but I held her firmly.

With her palm on my chest, I guided her hand along the middle of my chest, directly down my six pack, slowly making its way to my monster. Realizing what I was about to do, she began wrestling her hand from out my reach, and I smiled at her. Easing myself forward so I could speak in her ear, I instantly released her hand.

"This is what happens when you got a smart ass mouth." Without warning, I put my hand between her legs and squeezed her pussy, and I swore I heard her moan softly before she roughly shoved my hand away.

Hmmm, it's either Destiny doesn't have a man, or if she does, that nigga ain't hitting it right, I thought to myself as I began walking away from her.

"'Dingo, she's the only one that gets a lap dance?" I turned to the voice that spoke and made eye contact with the familiar face at the table. *Damn, this was Destiny's friend?* This chick was always in the club. I thought she told me her name was Julissa. I tried to give her a private dance one time, and she was begging me to fuck her. One thing I didn't ever do was fuck any of these females from the audience. I'd heard stories from some of the other male dancers, and fucking these female fans, well, that shit usually came back to bite you in the ass. Plus, that wasn't really my thing.

Julissa had a few hundred-dollar bills waving at me, so I decided to go ahead and give her thirsty ass a dance so I could make my paper.

CHAPTER THREE

Destiny

After receiving that lap dance from Trent, I was breathing as if I were having some type of asthma attack.

A stripper! That rude, obnoxious jackass who was a mechanic by day was also a stripper by night! What in the hell?

"Bitch! Spill the tea on how you knew that stripper, 'Dingo!'" Jamika cracked as we made our way toward her car about an hour after. I cut my eyes at her because she knew fully well I didn't know Trent like that.

"Ugh! Girl, he was the one that took care of the problem I was having with my car this morning. He's rude as hell, Jamika! No surprise he's a stripper!" I was lying through my teeth. I was shocked out of my mind, seeing Trent on that stage. He wasn't what I thought a stripper would look like.

He looked more like your average dope boy than an exotic dancer to me—all those tattoos on his arms, the piercings in his nose, his well-maintained beard, and a stank attitude to match, Trent was your regular dope boy from the block.

"Well, he sure seemed like he was enjoying giving you that lap dance." I felt my face flush as images of Trent gyrating on my lap flashed through my mind. The way his dick was pressing against my stomach and my lap—I was almost certain he had some type of surgery done to get his dick the length that it was. There was no way in hell one man could have been blessed with all that dick.

"Ppff, please, Jamika, 'Dingo gives everyone a lap dance. She ain't so special." Did I mention that I didn't like this trick Julissa? I scowled at her as we reached Jamika's 2005 Honda, which I nicknamed Betsy.

Julissa and Jamika met about three or four months ago in one of the local nightclubs. They actually both got into a fight with one of the girls at the club, and they beat her ass. They had been friends ever since. I, personally, didn't trust Julissa one bit.

Julissa always acted as if she was the only one who deserved to get any type of attention whenever we went out. That was one of the reasons I didn't like her ass.

"Julissa, girl, stop hating. Destiny didn't even have to pay for her dance like you did. She got that shit for free." Jamika chuckled as we all climbed in her car. I sat in the back while her prostitute friend sat up front.

My thoughts drifted back to Trent as Jamika attempted to start her car. My pussy was pulsing, thinking about the way he grabbed between my legs, and I shamelessly moaned as he did. I was acting as if I didn't have a man. Miguel was more than enough man for me. He may not have been working with an Anaconda like Trent, but he got the job done.

Still, I couldn't help but wonder what it would be like to have a man like Trent in the bedroom. *I bet he'd make me cum just by looking at me.*

I shook my head because I had no idea where those type of thoughts were coming from. It was only then I realized that Jamika's car wouldn't start.

"Shit! I keep telling Khalil he needs to get this car fixed."

I rolled my eyes so hard, sitting in that back seat. I was surprised they didn't get stuck in the back of my head. Khalil was Jamika's good-for-nothing baby daddy, whom I despised more than I did Julissa. Khalil took Jamika to hell and back only to drag her back to hell again. This nigga had done it all from cheating to getting other females pregnant and denying it. He even went to jail a couple times, yet Jamika stuck by his side. I didn't know why.

I honestly thought Jamika had low self-esteem. She was a dark-skinned sister that just happened to be what some people may call overweight. To me, Jamika was just perfect. I'd told her that so many times, but it just seemed to pass through one ear and out the other.

"Jamika, you know Khalil ain't about to do shit but run hoes out in the streets," Julissa said as she waved her hand around, her false nails about to poke Jamika's eye out.

"Now what we finna do?" Jamika kept turning the key in the ignition, but it refused to start. Groaning loudly, she slapped the steering wheel. I was about to take my phone out to call Miguel to come get us, even though I didn't want to, when Jamika spoke up.

"Aye, didn't you say he was a mechanic?" Jamika asked as she nudged her head, looking out into the parking lot. Following her eyes to see what she was staring at, I saw Trent making his way out the club with a backpack slung over his shoulder.

"Oh, hell no, Jamika. We not about to ask him for help." I shook my head. The last thing I needed was to see him face to face again.

"Forget you, Destiny. I'm not about to sit out here all night."

Before I could get another word out, Jamika jumped out the car and shouted out to Trent as she waved her arms wildly.

Julissa began fixing her hair and makeup as I sat in silence in the backseat.

"Oh, he's coming over!" Julissa shrieked excitedly as she clapped her hands together. Looking up slowly, sure enough, Trent and Jamika were heading toward Jamika's car. And all I wished for was the ground to open up and swallow me whole.

Ignoring both Julissa and me, he stood next to Jamika as she tried starting the car again. I sat there, looking at Trent as he casually leaned on the driver's door.

"Your battery's dead," he said dryly as I took in his appearance. Gone was the ridiculous shred of cloth he performed in early, replaced with a pair of black slim-fit jeans, a plain white vest, and a pair of Gucci slides on his feet.

"Can you fix it?" Jamika pleaded.

"Nope, don't have any jumper cables." I swore I wasn't making this shit up. But Trent's rude ass turned and began walking away. He was about to leave us there—three women… alone and stranded.

"Trent! So you're just gonna leave us!" I didn't even mean to say anything, but it was too late now.

I opened the car door and bolted after him, grabbing his arm. He turned and faced me with the blankest expression on his handsome face.

"Lady—I mean, Destiny... the fuck do you want me to do? You and your friends need to call a taxi." I stood there, gawking at him, hardly able to believe my ears.

"The least you could do is offer us a ride home." He snorted loudly at me as if what I requested were the most preposterous thing he has ever heard.

"The fuck I am! Get the fuck outta here." And with those words, he turned and began walking away.

"You are so obnoxious!" I screamed at him, but he didn't even turn around to acknowledge me.

"Let me handle this," a voice beside me said. I turned around, and Julissa sauntered past me, making her way toward Trent.

Exhaling loudly, I walked back to Jamika, who was on her cell phone, screaming her lungs out at her man.

"I've been telling you to get it fixed for almost a month now! And now we're stuck out here!" she yelled into her cellphone at Khalil. I shook my head at her because, to me, she could do so much better than Khalil's annoying ass.

I looked on as Julissa spoke with Trent, occasionally touching his arm and twirling her weave between her fingers. I hated to admit it to myself, but I was somewhat a little jealous because Trent was obviously loving the attention he was getting from her. I could tell by the way he was smiling. I rolled my eyes in annoyance because, looking at Julissa, she would most definitely be someone like Trent's type.

She had a big-old booty, the kind that had you wondering if that shit was fake. She always wore the latest designer brand clothes, and her hair was always styled to perfection with those expensive weaves she always wore. I sighed softly to myself as Jamika got off the phone, and Julissa came walking back over to us.

"You good?" I turned to my girl, who looked like she was about to burst out crying.

"I'm good. One day, I'll get the courage to leave that nigga," Jamika mumbled to herself, and I reached over and gave her a friendly hug as we stood, leaning on her car.

"Come on. He's gon' take us home," Julissa said as she reached for her belongings in the front seat of the car. Not even bothering to say anything, because we were just happy that we weren't stranded anymore, Jamika and I took our stuff from her car, and all three of us walked briskly over to Trent's black Audi. Clearly, being a stripper was worth it, seeing the type of car he was driving and all. He was already sitting behind the wheel with the engine running.

Opening the back door, Jamika and I were about to climb in, while Julissa made her way to sit in the front.

"Nah, let big mouth sit up front," Trent said as he waved his hand at Julissa as he turned around to watch me with a smirk on his face.

"What?" Julissa asked, sounding irritated as hell at what Trent just requested.

"Destiny, come sit up front with me."

Jamika and I made eye contact, as I was a little shocked that he'd rather I sat in the front seat and not Julissa.

"Girl, just go so we can get the hell out of here," Jamika said as she sat down in the back seat. Exhaling softly because Trent was beginning to ride my last nerve, I made my way to the passenger side. Julissa was still standing at the door, looking pissed as I stood there, waiting for her to get the hell out of my way.

We stared at each other for a good few seconds before she sucked her teeth loudly at me, pushing past me to sit her ass in the back. Did I mention before that I didn't like that hoe?

Sitting down, I closed the door, refusing to even acknowledge Trent as I felt his eyes on me. I heard him chuckle as he drove off. My head stubbornly turned so I could look out the window.

"Bye, girl, call me when you get home," Jamika said as she made her way out the car. We already dropped Julissa off, and it was just Jamika and me. Something told me Trent deliberately left me for last.

"OK, I will. And go easy on Khalil." We laughed together as she made her way inside of her house.

Trent pulled off, and we drove in silence, as I had already given him directions to where I lived.

"So you enjoy watching men gyrating in your face?" The first words out of his mouth since we left the club, and he had to insult me? Narrowing my eyes at him, I decided I wasn't even going to reply, so I looked away from him.

"How come you friends with that hoe, Julissa?" Well, that was one thing we agreed on—the fact that Julissa was a ho.

"She's not my friend. Jamika is. She and Jamika are friends." I saw him shake his head thoughtfully as if my answer pleased him.

"Why you out here stripping? Doesn't your job at the auto shop pay you enough?" I asked, turning my attention to him. His face concentrated on the road ahead, and his features looked relaxed as I eye raped him. He was no doubt a very handsome man, even with all those tattoos and his nose piercings. Everything seemed to work well for him. He licked his lips, and I felt my pussy twitch. I cursed myself and looked away.

"I got a big dick. Women like to see big dicks, so I might as well get paid for showing it off." His reply was so dry and straightforward that I couldn't help but laugh a little.

"Are you always so blunt?"

He shrugged his shoulders, and I shook my head as he turned onto my street.

"Besides, I'm saving my money for a business venture. When I have enough saved up, I'll quit. But for now, I'm Trent, the mechanic, by day and 'Dingo, the exotic dancer, by night." I pointed my house out to him, and he pulled up in front of my two-bedroom home that I inherited after my father passed away.

Trent definitely wasn't what one would expect a male stripper would look like; he wasn't insanely muscular. He had a nice body on him, but nothing screamed stripper.

"Well, Trent by day and 'Dingo by night, thanks for dropping my girls and myself home." I smiled genuinely at him even though he was an ass at first.

"It's cool. Tell your friend she can come get her car tomorrow at about five in the afternoon. I'll have it fixed by then." He turned to me, his gaze roaming over my body. The body-hugging, short dress I wore suddenly felt too tight. Let me hurry up and leave before this man devoured me with his eyes.

I attempted to open the door, but it was locked. Turning to Trent, I raised my eyebrow at him as I waited for him to unlock it. Never taking his eyes off me, he flipped the button, and I heard the door unlock, and I pulled on the handle, only Trent locked it again.

Totally unamused, I sighed loudly in frustration.

"Quit playing, Trent," I said, barely recognizing my own voice. It was husky as hell.

"You got a man, Destiny?" He began playing with his beard as if he were deep in thought.

"Yes, I do. He was the one that bought my BMW that you fixed earlier." I didn't even know why I felt the need to express that Miguel had purchased my car.

Licking his lips slow and seductively, still stroking his beard, Trent smiled slowly. "Let that nigga know he's about to lose you."

Speechless as fuck as Trent leaned into me, I held my breath, too scared to even move as Trent pushed his body against mine. Our faces were mere inches apart. Our eyes locked with each other's as he reached for the door and gently opened it.

"Bye, Destiny," he said as he put his lips against my ear. His warm breath brushed against my neck, the masculine scent of his cologne invading my nostrils.

Not even sure when I climbed out of his car, I closed the door as Trent drove off, my tongue still heavy from shock.

An hour after, I was lying in bed with my legs spread open as I pleasured myself with my bullet vibrator. Visions of Trent played in my head as I gripped the sheets, moaning loudly, my orgasm close.

"Aaahhh!" I screamed as I came hard. My clit felt painful and sensitive as I continued making circular motions with my vibrator.

Trent's smiling face was all that I saw later on as I drifted off to sleep.

CHAPTER FOUR

Trent

"The fuck," I said into the silence of my room as my phone began ringing. It was almost three in the morning. Grabbing the phone from under my pillow, I frowned when I saw the name on the screen… Tricia.

Swiping the phone, I answered the call. "Hey, baby sis, what's good?"

"Trent." The way she said my name as if she were breathless, I sat upright in my bed.

"What's up, baby sis? You good? What's wrong?" I was already out of my bed, shuffling through my drawer for clothes.

"Can you come get me, please?" she asked as she began sobbing through the phone.

I let her know to sit tight, and I was on my way. I wasted no time throwing on a pair of sweatpants and plain black T-shirt. Grabbing up my keys for my ride, I made my way out of my home to rescue my sister once again.

Clenching my jaw as I drove some fifteen minutes to where my sister lived, I kept shaking my head. My sister was six years younger than me, but to me, a twenty-two-year-old should have more sense than she did.

I couldn't put all the blame on her, though. Sometimes, I believed she was just a product of her environment. My sister and I grew up in the most abusive household one could imagine. Both of our parents were abusive, my father being the worse. We would get our butts beat for the simplest of things from spilling a glass of milk to not putting away our toys or even if we didn't finish eating all our dinner.

You name it, we got our asses whooped for it. Our mother was just as evil as our father. She didn't beat us as much, but she sure as hell never tried to help when we were being dealt with. So she was just as bad in my book.

From the moment Tricia started dating niggas, she would always end up with the ones who would use her as a punching bag. And of course, since our mother and father didn't give a shit, I would always be the one to save her from these Mike Tyson niggas.

Our childhood was rough, and we dealt with the shit happening at home differently. Tricia started having sex at a young age, and I would always get into fights on the street, in schools, or at part-time jobs that I sometimes took. You name a place, and I was sure I probably beat some niggas ass there already.

The only good thing that my father ever did was teach me how to fix cars. That's where my love for vehicles started—my father. Everything else, I learned on the streets or from females.

I never looked at my dick as a blessing or anything like that. But the first time I had sex at the tender age of thirteen, that woman... yes woman, thought I was blessed, and my dick was a gift from God himself.

Her name was Clarissa. She was seventeen years old and lived just a couple houses down from us. She had a nice, peanut-butter complexion, and she was thick as hell with a big old Sir Mix-A-Lot booty. Clarissa would come by whenever both my parents weren't at home just to make sure my sister and I were OK. There was this one day that I had just gotten out of the shower, and Clarissa walked in on me by accident as I towel-dried myself. Let's just say she was very impressed with my package. She closed the bathroom door, and just like that, she got on her knees and started sucking my dick. She told me my big dick had to be a gift from God himself.

Eventually, we started fucking. She taught me a lot—even how to eat pussy. Yup, Clarissa and I did it all. Nobody ever found out about us, and just a few days shy of her eighteenth birthday, she came to me and said she was moving—something about her boyfriend wanting them to live together. I never saw her again after she left, not even one time.

Pulling up at my sister's apartment, I could hear the screams and yelling from all the way outside. Before I got out of the car, I took a few deep breaths because fighting my sister's battles with these knuckleheads she kept getting involved with landed me in jail a few times.

But I didn't feel like going to jail tonight, so I decided, before I walked in there, to keep it chill. Making my way up the flight of stairs,

I stopped at her apartment door.

"Get the fuck out!" Tricia screamed as I put my hand up and knocked the door. Quite frankly, I was getting tired of always rescuing her. The only reason why I kept getting involved was my four-year-old niece.

"Bitch, fuck you! I pay the bills up in here!"

I exhaled loudly as I knocked on the door. I couldn't even remember the name of the loser she shacked up with this time.

"Tricia!" I yelled as I pounded loudly on the front door. Before I could knock again, the door flung open, leaving me surprised that they even heard me.

"Oh, good, hurry up and get your crazy ass sister out my apartment."

Completely ignoring him, seeing how I couldn't even remember his name, I made my way inside, rushing by him.

I glared angrily at my sister wearing nothing but a pair of boy shorts and a sports bra on. She smiled when she saw me... but I didn't.

"Yo, where's Heaven-Leigh?" I asked, pointing my finger at her. She already had a couple of bags packed that sat at her feet.

"She's in there." Tricia pointed to a room, and I quickly made my way over to that direction. My niece was lying down on a mattress on the floor with her eyes closed tight and her hands covering her ears. The only time my emotions ever got the better of me was when I saw this little human right here. And seeing her like this, lying on a dirty mattress on the floor, curled up in a fetal position with her hands blocking the noise of two adults arguing, had me mad as fuck.

As I made my way to her, she opened her eyes and came to me. I bent and scooped her up in my arms.

"Baby girl, you alright?" I spoke softly to her as I kissed the top of her head.

"Mommy is mad at Duane again." Her lower lip trembled as she spoke as I put her on her feet, I told her to wait for me to get her mommy, and then we were going over to my house. She smiled, shaking her head excitedly as I made my way back outside.

Stepping back into the living room, I saw Tricia up in Duane's face, arguing. I knew his name now thanks to my niece. I walked up to Tricia and grabbed her by her elbow, forcing her to turn to me.

"What the fuck is wrong with you?" I asked, my jaw tight as I glared angrily at her. Her left eye was slightly swollen and red, letting me know she had gotten hit.

"Heaven is in there crying and shit, and you out here acting a motherfuckin' fool! Get yo' shit and let's go!" I barked at her, releasing her arm as I went back to get my niece. "Tired of you and these lame ass niggas you keep putting yourself with, Tricia!" I yelled at her as I made my way to the front door with Heaven-Leigh safe in my arms. Without saying anything else, I left the apartment, not caring if she was behind me or not. The most important person was in my arms.

****

"You ready for your first day of school, Heaven?" I looked in the rearview mirror at my niece as she sat quietly in the back seat. Two weeks had passed since I took her and my sister over to my house. I let Tricia know she was not about to leave with my niece unless she had another place to live, because she wasn't about to go back to that abusive nigga's place.

"Yes, Uncle Trent, I'm ready."

I smiled at her as I pulled into the drop-off zone for a private school that I enrolled her in. I didn't mind paying for her tuition as long as she got an education. Even if it meant I had to dip out of the money I saved up for my future business plans.

We were a little late because Heaven-Leigh decided at the last minute that she wanted her hair in pigtails and not the cornrow style her mother did.

Making our way down the hall, I was instructed by the principal that I had to take her to the classroom that was three doors down. The door was closed, and I heard the kids reciting their alphabet. I knocked on the door twice and waited. Heaven and I looked at each other. I was feeling nervous as hell like if it was my first day instead of hers.

When the door opened, I promise I almost pissed in my pants.

It was Destiny, and she was looking fly as hell in her black and white, pinstriped pants suit, a black pair of stilettos, and her nerdy glasses on her face with her hair pulled to the top of her head in a curly fro.

"Trent?" she asked, looking all types of confused.

"Destiny? You're a teacher?" I asked incredulously as we stood there, staring at each other.

"What is that supposed to mean?" She folded her arms as she if she was daring me to answer.

"You're a teacher that likes to visit strip clubs." Her mouth dropped open then, and I chuckled softly.

"Anyway, this little human here is my niece, Heaven-Leigh Bishop. Say hello to Miss..." I stretched out the word miss as I waited for Destiny to fill in the blanks.

"Um, Miss Charles," Destiny said as she smiled sweetly down at my niece.

"Nice to meet you, Heaven-Leigh, and that's a very pretty name." I stood in silence as Destiny took Heaven to her seat, helping her get settled in.

Destiny turned and made her way to where I stood at the door. Holding on to my elbow, she led me outside and closed the door softly behind her.

"You again?" she asked as she smirked at me.

"Me again," I repeated, and we both laughed. Destiny looked down at her high heels as if she were suddenly shy.

"So you're an uncle?"

"I'm an uncle, yes. Nice to see you again, by the way." I eyed her slowly as I always did because this woman was fine. She possessed curves, smooth skin, curly natural hair, and lips that looked like they could suck the hell out of a dick.

I smiled as my thoughts strayed, and my eyes remained focused on her lips.

"Well... um, I better get back in there," she said nervously, and I was able to focus on her face again. "Are you the only one that's going to be dropping and picking up Heaven-Leigh?" she asked with her hand on the doorknob.

"Why? Do you want me to be the only one that's picking up and dropping her off?" I took a small step toward her because I was enjoying the way I made her nervous. It let me know she was somewhat attracted to me.

She giggled. "No, it's just we need to know who we're allowed to let the child leave with." She bit her lower lip as we were now so close I could feel her body heat.

"So you don't want to see me again… Miss Charles? Did you tell your boyfriend what I said? That he's about to lose you?" Before, when I told her that, I was just talking shit to be an ass, but now, I actually thought I was sort of interested in Destiny. Something told me she had a lot of freak in her, and I wanted to find out my damn self.

"Destiny?" We both turned around at the sound of her name, and I was greeted with another familiar face—her chocolate friend from the club.

I scrunched up my face in disbelief. "Shawty, you work here too?" I looked from Destiny then back to her friend and found this shit hilarious.

"Yo, both of you better not teach my niece about visiting no damn strip club when she's older." They narrowed their eyes at me, and I decided to make my retreat before Destiny began to chew my ass out.

"I'll see you later, Miss Charles." I smiled at her before turning to leave, and her friend smirked at me.

Operation: Get Destiny, was now in progress, I thought to myself as I made my way to my car.

CHAPTER FIVE

Destiny

"Mmmm, right there, Miguel." I moaned loudly, grabbing a fistful of my man's hair as I grinded my pussy into his face. Miguel's head game was always on point. He took his time and made love to my clit. He was never rough with me.

But… just as I was about to cum, he would always move away, which always got me mad, but I never said anything. He said the juices women excreted when they came was unhealthy for a man to drink— which was the most craziest shit I've heard in my life.

"You know I love you, right?" he said as he positioned himself to enter me. Looking up at him, I shook my head as I inched my hips forward because for some reason, I needed to feel him inside, like now.

"Yes, I know, and I love you to. Please, just put it in." My and Miguel's sex talk was a bit more proper than most. I used to say really dirty things to him during sex, but he told me I needed to stop acting ghetto. So I never did it again. Now we had a more formal way of speaking during sex.

"Hmmm, you missed me, huh, Destiny?" he asked as he pushed

his dick inside me. I groaned loudly as I grabbed ahold of his shoulders and raised my hips eagerly to meet his thrusts. He wasn't moving in the speed I needed, so I put my hand on his waist and began rocking him forward faster.

"Slow down, baby, or you'll make me cum too fast." I rolled my eyes so hard. Thank God the room was dark, so he couldn't see. This was problem number two. Miguel usually lasted only a of couple minutes.

I was talking about, he came so fast I didn't even have time to go in any other position. Miguel was nothing but a premature ejaculator. But I worked with him because I loved him.

"Oh, oh, oh, God… Destiny!" And just as fast as it started, it was now over. Miguel emptied his load in the condom he wore and rolled off of me to lie on his side. This nigga was breathing so hard you would have sworn we just fucked for a good hour. He didn't even have the decency to allow me to cum.

"I love you, babe," he said as he kissed my shoulder and cuddled up against my back. I didn't answer as I waited for his breathing to regulate, letting me know he was asleep.

As I heard his light snores, I removed his hand from my torso and climbed out the bed, picking up a blanket and my phone from off the nightstand as I made my way to my living room.

Sitting on the love seat in the dark, I curled my feet under me and bit my lip in as I swiped my screen to unlock it. I smiled like a schoolgirl as I saw I had over twenty WhatsApp messages.

Clicking on the icon, I saw all of the messages were from Trent. This had been going on for a while now. The first day he dropped off his niece, he asked for my number that afternoon when he came to get Heaven-Leigh. He claimed he needed it if his niece missed school, and he wanted to know what we did in class.

Even though I knew that was bullshit, against my better judgement, I gave it to him. And we had been in constant contact since then, which was about a week ago.

I smiled as I read each and every one of his messages. He was about to go on stage and perform, and I asked to see what he was wearing. He took a picture of himself in his costume, and I bit into my lower lip to keep from drooling. Tonight, he was dressed in the usual loin cloth that barely hid his blessing, and his chest was oiled up, his tattoos glistening.

Do you like it? he messaged, and I smiled as I tapped on the screen to reply.

It's nice, I like it, I replied, waiting for him to respond.

Would you like to see what's underneath? I bit into my lip again as I thought about what I should say. It was the first time he ever asked me that, and Miguel flashed across my mind. I did feel bad about what I was doing behind his back, but one little picture couldn't hurt, right?

Ok... was my reply as I held my breath. When the message came up with the picture icon, I started biting my nails nervously. Closing my eyes, I tapped the screen and slowly opened my eyes again.

I was motherfuckin' floored.

"Oh my God," I whispered softly as my eyes took its sweet time to look at what Trent was working with. Now this was a big motherfucker, looked like a fucking womb shifter; it even had a lil' curve at the end.

The tip was pink and shiny, the length was filled with big juicy veins, and the thickness of it was like a full-grown cucumber. My mouth started to salivate.

You like what you see Destiny? The message popped up, and I began tapping the screen to reply.

Yes... yes I do. This was so wrong. I paused because I swore I heard footsteps. I listened to see if it was Miguel, and my ears were up like antennas. I realized it was nothing as Trent sent me another message.

Can I come over after my shift? I knew exactly what he wanted to come over for, and I was not ready for that. I began tapping at my screen, faster this time.

My boyfriend is sleeping over tonight. Thinking Trent needed a gentle reminder that I was taken, I sent the message. I waited for his reply, but one never came. I wrinkled my forehead, wondering if he was upset with me. I knew he read my message—the tick was blue—so why no reply.

Trent???? I typed, hoping he would answer.

"Destiny?"

I almost jumped out of my skin when I heard Miguel's voice behind me. I quickly returned to my home screen as I turned to face him. Miguel was a handsome man. He looked like a younger version of Blair Underwood with a curly fro and a nice, medium-built body. He stood, staring at me, in only a black pair of boxers.

"Hey, baby, I couldn't sleep," I lied as I stood up from off the sofa, wrapping the blanket around my naked body.

"Come on. Let's go back to bed," he said as I forced a smile, and he held his hand out to me. I placed my hand in his, and we made our way back to the bedroom. My hand grasped the phone firmly, my mind heavy in thought, wondering if Trent would reply to me or not.

Miguel pulled me against his chest as he wrapped his arm protectively around me. I settled into him and decided that I should put an end to whatever it was I had going on with Trent.

The only problem with that was I couldn't stop thinking about him.

CHAPTER SIX

Trent

Jealousy was a word I would never use to describe myself. But when Destiny sent me that message saying that she had her nigga over for the night, I almost threw my fucking phone against the wall. Never in my life had a female gotten me so upset that I felt like leaving the club and making my way over to her house.

What the fuck was wrong with me? Destiny was spoken for. I knew that, so why would the thought of her nigga laying up in bed with her get me so angry?

"Ugghh." I groaned loudly as my phone alarmed, letting me know it was time for me to get up and get ready for work and drop Heaven off at school. Wiping the palm of my hand vigorously across my face, I was about to sit up in my bed, when suddenly, a hand began caressing my naked chest.

Shit! I almost forget this trick was here. What was her name again? Oh yeah, Julissa.

"Mmmm, baby, where you going?" She lowered her hand to my crotch, but I quickly swatted it away.

See, what had happened was Destiny got me so mad that I needed to release some of my tension, so when I saw Julissa in the crowd, I remembered she owed a nigga. That night when her homegirl's car refused to start, and I dropped them off to their homes, Julissa said she would do me the honors of sucking my dick. So I obliged, not only to get my dick sucked, but because I would have gotten to be around Destiny again.

"A nigga gotta work. But I guess you don't know anything about that," I cracked at her as I got up from off the bed. I began getting myself together to have a bath.

"My man takes care of me, so I don't have to work." I stared at her with a dumbfounded look on my face *What did she just say?*

"Julissa, you got a nigga?"

She looked at me as if I were stupid. "Of course I got a man, Trent." She scoffed at me, and I shook my head. Some women were foul as hell. "So we not going to give it another try?"

I wanted to laugh in her face, but it was too early in the morning to be so mean. I know you all are probably thinking that I fucked Julissa, but you guys would be wrong. As I stated before, she promised me to suck my dick, which was the reason I foolishly brought her back to my apartment. It turned out that she couldn't suck a dick to save her life. She was so bad at it that I pushed her off me, telling her I was suddenly not feeling well.

"Nah, I'm straight, but you need to bounce before my niece wakes up." Not giving her a chance to reply, I picked up her dress and tossed it to her on the bed before turning to make my way to the bathroom.

"Tricia, you are looking for a new apartment, right?" I questioned my baby sister as she pranced around in her underwear, making breakfast for Heaven.

"And put some fucking clothes on. This ain't the motherfuckin' Hyatt." She cut her eyes at me, and Heaven wagged her finger at me.

"Oooh, Uncle Trent, you said a bad word." Sometimes, I'd forget that I needed to watch what I said around Heaven.

"My bad, Heaven," I said as I bent and kissed her cheek.

"Who you telling, Trent? Don't think I didn't hear somebody in your room last night," Tricia said, smirking at me as she packed her daughter's lunch. Thankfully, Julissa left before either my sister or niece woke up.

"Nah, Tricia, you don't get to question me. This my crib. C'mon, Heaven, let's roll." Stepping into my room, I picked up my car keys, opened my top drawer, and grabbed a little gift I wanted to give to Destiny when I saw her this morning.

I needed to let her know once and for all that I wanted her to be mine and mine only. I knew I may have sounded a bit bold, but that was the type of nigga I was. When I saw something I wanted, I went out and grabbed it.

Usually, I wasn't the type to get emotionally attached to any female. I was the hit-it-and-quit type of dude. I personally never stuck around long enough for any female to get attached to me; after all, I was an exotic dancer. Which female out here was about to take me seriously?

"Miss Charles, can I have a word with you?" Heaven waved at

me as she walked to take her seat in Destiny's class. Destiny was seated behind her desk, waiting for all of her students to arrive, as class wasn't about to start just yet.

Looking over at me, she seemed to be annoyed as she got up and walked over in my direction. Closing the door behind her, she folded her arms under her breasts. As always, I greedily examined her and smiled to myself when I saw she was wearing a red skirt suit today with a pair of black pumps. Her lil' nerdy glasses sat firmly on her face, but I was happy she wore a skirt because that would make it easier to execute my plan.

"What do you want, Trent? And why didn't you message me back last night? I know you read it… You are so obnoxious and ru—"

I held my hands out at her because she was going all the way off. "Chill, Destiny, damn. Let's go somewhere and talk. Let me explain."

She breathed out in frustration as she continued to glare at me. She was not budging, so I decided to take a different approach.

"Look, at least show me where I can use the bathroom. I gotta pee." I held onto the crotch of my pants for emphasis. Rolling her eyes at me, she unfolded her arms and placed them at her side.

"We don't really allow visitors to use the bathrooms, Trent." Destiny was really making shit hard for a nigga.

"So you gon' just let me piss in my drawers?" I glared at her, playing my role as if I were upset.

Exhaling softly, she grabbed my elbow. "I guess you can use the janitor's restroom. C'mon." I smiled wickedly to myself as she led me down the corridor. Her ass bounced around in her work suit, so I got an eyeful as I walked behind her. I adjusted my monster as he began reacting to Destiny's presence.

She stopped suddenly and turned to face me.

"You can go ahead and use this one."

I smiled at her and slowly licked my lips. She furrowed her eyebrows as if she were trying to understand my reaction. I turned around, looking over my shoulder, making sure no one else was around, and I turned the door knob and peeked inside. The bathroom had a toilet that looked fairly clean and a small sink to the side.

Grabbing ahold of Destiny's hand, I pulled her inside and closed the door, locking it behind us.

"Trent, what the hell are doing? Open this door and let me the fuck out." She gritted her teeth as she spoke, her nostrils flaring, but she wasn't intimidating me in the least.

I began taking small steps toward her, and she began walking backward in the direction of the sink.

"Do all teachers talk like that? Cussing and shit?" I asked as I reached into my jeans pocket for what I had planned for her.

"Do you think this funny?" she asked as she stopped walking because she had nowhere else to go. "Anybody could walk by and hear us. You're so fucking childish." She attempted to walk past me, but I quickly grabbed her by her wrist.

"Where you think you going?" I tightened the grip on her wrist and backed her ass up against the door. It was then she looked down at my hand, trying to focus on what I held.

"What did I tell you, Destiny?"

She looked at me confusedly.

"Didn't I tell you to let your nigga know he was about to lose you? What was he doing over at your place last night… huh?" Taking a hold of her other wrist, I pinned her hands above her head with my one hand, jamming her against the bathroom door.

Her chest began rising and falling. Her breathing was erratic, and her pupils grew darker with lust. Oh, I had Destiny exactly where I wanted her. I smiled at her and licked my lips.

"Are you crazy? You can't expect me to leave my man just because you want me to, Trent."

"You not understanding me, Destiny," I said as I took my hand, placing it at the hem of her skirt that was right above her knees. I slowly began lifting it over her thigh.

"Trent," she said breathlessly as she heard the buzzing of the vibrator, my little gift that I walked with just for her. I was about to show Destiny that this game was over.

"What are you about to do with that? This is fucking crazy … Let me get back to teach my class." She looked sexy as fuck as she tried her best to control what she was obviously feeling for me.

Ignoring her, I held the small vibrator between my index and middle finger and began running it against the inside of her thigh, and she instantly began to tremble.

"You gon' tell that nigga what I said?" I inched my finger closer to the outside of her panties. Destiny's mouth was slightly open as her breath came out in short gasps.

"Trent… please, I can't."

That definitely was not the answer I wanted to hear, so she was about to be punished. Inching my face closer to hers, I gently brushed my lips against hers, biting into her lower lip before putting my lips to her ear.

"I don't think you understanding." Taking my fingers, the vibrating device making a low buzzing noise, I ran it along the outside of her panties.

Destiny took a loud intake of breath as she tried to free her wrist from being held above her head.

"You gon' tell him, Destiny?" I whispered hoarsely to her, my dick hard as a rock as it strained against my zipper. Pulling her underwear to one side, I placed the vibrator against her wet clit.

"Aahhh… Trent." She moaned softly as she pushed her hips toward my hand. The way she grinded on my fingers, I would have sworn her man didn't handle her right last night.

"You like that?" I removed my face from her ear so that I could now stare in her eyes from behind her glasses. They were barely open as she fought to breathe.

"That nigga ever came by your work and made you cum like this?" I asked as I bit into her lower lip again. I adjusted the speed on the vibrator, making it go even faster, moving it in a circular motion against her exposed flesh.

"Answer me, or I'll stop… You gon' tell that nigga?" I could tell she was close by the way her breathing picked up, and her hips started bucking wildly as she struggled to free her wrists.

Then I stopped completely.

Her eyes flew open, and she glared at me in obvious anger. I licked my lips slowly and smiled.

"Fucking let me go, Trent." She pulled angrily, trying to free her wrists. Oh, she was big mad.

"Nah, answer me… You gon' tell him?" Unable to resist, I bent and kissed her lips, and she wasted no time to open her mouth, allowing me to clash my tongue with hers. Resuming what I started, I placed the vibrator on her clit.

"Yesss… I'll tell him," she finally replied breathlessly against my lips.

"Try not to scream," I told her, and she had a look of confusion on her face. I released her wrists and got on my knees between her thighs. I devoured her pussy in my mouth, flicking my tongue with lightning speed quickness against her clit, and she exploded in record time in my mouth.

She stifled her screams by shoving four of her fingers into her mouth.

Destiny tasted like sugar, I kid you not, as I hungrily lapped up her release in my mouth. Putting her underwear back in its rightful place, I stood up and turned the vibrator off and stared at her as she struggled to get herself together.

Shoving my hand down my pants because big boy thought he

was about to come out and play, I also tried to bring myself back to normal.

"It's time for you to go back to your class."

She adjusted her skirt, and then fixed her lil' nerdy glasses I loved so much on her face. She looked at me and narrowed her eyes as if she was about to speak but changed her mind.

Grabbing ahold of the door, I unlocked it and pushed it open, and we almost walked straight into her chocolate friend.

"Destiny?"

"Jamika!"

They both looked at each other for a couple seconds before Jamika raised her eyebrows at Destiny and smirked.

"Hey, Trent," she said and began laughing, "Um, Destiny, your kids are acting up, so I came to find you." She continued smirking, and I decided that this was a good time to make my retreat.

"See you later, Miss Charles, and remember what I said." I glared at her before turning to leave.

Shoving the vibrator in my pocket, I made my way to the auto shop. There was something about Destiny that I couldn't get enough of, and I for damn sure didn't want anyone else to have her.

CHAPTER SEVEN

Jamika

I stood up in the full-length mirror and stared at my reflection. I raised my arm and shook it, and it jiggled. I raised my arms above my head to try to make breasts appear perkier. I inspected the stretchmarks on my stomach, my proof that I carried my now two-year-old son. I tried to smooth out the cellulite on my thighs by pulling my skin upward. I even looked between my thighs that were now a little darker in complexion because my thighs rubbed when I walked. I sighed softly, feeling defeated.

Grabbing my towel from the bed, I wrapped it around my naked body and headed to the bathroom to have a shower. I tried really hard not to feel sorry for myself, but I had good days and horrible days; this was a horrible day.

Turning on the shower, I stood under the water, hoping the warm spray would somehow ease my stress. I was a twenty-eight-year-old Black woman who felt like fifty on most days.

I was the mother of a two-year-old energetic child, whom I loved more than life itself. I should be happy, right? I should be grateful that

I had a healthy son, and I had air in my lungs... Wrong—I was fucking miserable.

I hated my body. Childbirth had done a number on it. My stomach was no longer flat, and my breasts always needed the help of a bra because gravity had taken over. I felt ugly inside and outside. My son's father didn't do anything to help my insecurities. Hell, he was the reason I had them in the first place.

Khalil and I had been together since high school. He was my first everything, and he swore we would be together forever. The only problem was Khalil couldn't keep his dick in his pants like 90 percent of the time.

I'd had to deal with females calling my phone at all hours of the night, asking me if I knew my man was laid up in bed with them. I had to deal with minding my own business in the supermarket and some random bitch snickering at me with her friends, saying she was fucking my man.

I'd dealt with infidelity after infidelity with Khalil, and sometimes, I would say to myself, *I've had enough, and I'm going to leave him.* But I never did. I mean, who'd want me, an overweight mother of one? Who'd want me?

Khalil had two other kids on the outside that I only found out about recently—one, he fathered by my very own cousin. I was so ashamed I didn't even reveal that to my best friend Destiny. The only person I told was Julissa.

Julissa and I had a little bit more in common than Destiny. We were both a little more streetwise than her, so there were things that

I just felt more comfortable about discussing with Julissa than with Destiny.

Sometimes, I secretly wished I had Destiny's life. I wished that I could be as pretty as her with all the men falling at my feet. I'd seen men tripping over themselves just to get her attention. But I wasn't that lucky. I was stuck in my loveless relationship just wishing someone would come and love me the way I hoped for.

"Jamika!"

I exhaled loudly at the sound of Khalil's voice. He sounded annoyed about something, as always. Not even bothering to answer, I washed the soap off my body, getting ready to climb out the shower.

"Jamika!" he screamed at me again as he threw open the bathroom door. "Don't you hear me calling your ass?" I turned the shower off and took the towel to dry myself off, and all the while, I was still silent.

I climbed out the shower, and Khalil glared at me as if I took the last piece of chicken from the oven.

"What's wrong, Khalil?" I asked dryly as I walked by him to get into our bedroom.

"I need to get something from the corner store real quick. Lend me a hundred."

The nerve of this nigga right here, I thought as I looked him over.

"You hollering like a madman all because you want me to give you some money?" I stared at him, stopping from applying lotion to my legs.

Now don't get me wrong; when I looked at Khalil, I could see why the females were tripping over their own feet to get with him. This nigga had not changed much since high school. He and Michael B. Jordan could be twins. Khalil had a nice pair of full lips that when you saw them, the only thing that came to mind was how good he could probably eat pussy. His body type was that of a basketballer—nice, firm, and hard... Yup, the ladies sure loved him, and he loved them right back.

"You giving it to me, or nah? A nigga don't have time for all your lip tonight."

Disrespectful ass, I said to myself as I walked over to where my handbag was to grab the money for him. Taking the bill out, I placed it in his outstretched hand, and he quickly grabbed it and shoved it in his pocket.

"Where's Kaden at?" he enquired about our son.

"He's asleep," I replied, removing the towel from around me as I took an oversized T-shirt from my top drawer. Khalil looked away as if seeing me naked was some type of turnoff. I quickly threw the T-shirt over my head to cover my body, fearing that he would rudely comment about my fat stomach or chunky thighs.

"I'll be back in a few hours. Make me some fried chicken and mac and cheese for when I get back."

I gawked him as if he were insane. I just made mashed potatoes, corn on the cob, and baked chicken, and now he was asking for a completely different menu.

"Khalil, I cooked about an hour ago." I had a blank expression on my face because I knew he was about to complain.

"Yeah, but I don't want that. Just make what I asked for, aight."

His voice softened, and he closed the distance between us and kissed my cheek.

He turned and jogged out of the room, leaving to go visit one of his many female friends no doubt, *talking 'bout going to the corner store.* I knew better.

With a heavy heart, I walked out of the bedroom and decided to go check on our son; he was still sound asleep, and I bent down, kissing the top of his head.

Making my way to the kitchen to prepare the meal Khalil requested, I stopped and turned the TV on. Opening the refrigerator door, I pulled out the ingredients that I would need. In the distance, I heard an advertisement come on, one I'd heard many times before; but this time, I stopped and listened.

It was an ad for one of the local gyms. Focusing my attention on the screen, I listened as the narrator advertised a special they were having this month.

Maybe instead of always feeling sorry for myself, I should actually do something about my weight. As the number flashed across the screen, I grabbed up a pen and piece of paper from the kitchen counter and wrote it down.

I made a vow to myself right then and there that I was going to make a difference in my life; not even for Khalil to finally appreciate me again, but for me to start back loving myself. I was about to turn over a new leaf.

And when I got done getting my sexy back, Khalil was going to wish he would have treated me better.

CHAPTER EIGHT

Destiny

I sat there, daydreaming, in the quiet of the teacher's lounge as I nibbled on my salad. My mind drifted to Trent when he had me up against the door in the janitor's bathroom two days ago, the vibrator buzzing slowly against my clit, then Trent getting on his knees to finish the job with his hurricane tongue.

"Mmmm…" I smiled to myself, clamping my thighs together as my pussy began pulsing so much it damn near hurt.

I hadn't heard from him since. His sister dropped and picked Heaven-Leigh up from school the past two days. I, for one, wasn't about to message or call his ass, because I knew he was dead ass serious with me ending things with Miguel. Unfortunately, it wasn't that simple. I honestly cared deeply for Miguel; it was just… we grew apart.

He worked so much that I rarely got to spend any real time with him, and when we did, it was kinda boring and felt forced. We hardly went out and enjoyed each other's company, and then there was the issue with our love life.

I hadn't really had my share of men—just one boyfriend before

I met Miguel. My first boyfriend was more street savvy. His name was Terrence AKA Terror. My father hated the best bone in his body. Terror was all sorts of wrong. That nigga created havoc wherever he went, but his dick game was strong as fuck. He broke through my virgin skin, and after that, there was no turning back. He was the one that taught me to talk dirty during sex.

But when my father passed away, and I met Miguel, I knew if my father were still alive, he would have approved of Miguel. So maybe that was the true reason I got with him.

It was also the reason I would subject myself to his weak ass dick. The first couple times we had sex, I thought maybe it was just pure excitement that caused Miguel to cum as quickly as he did. But then I realized this motherfucker was clearly a premature ejaculator after it kept happening months after we started fucking.

To this day, I'd never brought it up with him. I figured if you loved somebody, you'd accept the good along with the bad. After meeting Trent, I knew it was only so long that I would be able to resist him, but I for damn sure would be trying to fight it.

"Hey, girl." Jamika walked in, bringing me out of my thoughts. I smiled at her as she sat next to me with her lunch bowl in hand.

"Hey, girl, what's good?" I asked her as she sat down and uncovered her bowl and began eating. Taking a look at the contents in her lunch bowl, I became curious.

"Well, look at you. You on a diet or something?" I enquired. I couldn't help being all up in her Kool-Aid as she began pecking at her salad.

"I just decided that I wanted to change my eating habits a bit, that's all."

I smiled at her because I was really impressed. "Well, go, Jamika; I'm proud of you, girl."

She smiled at me, and I smiled back.

"Anyway, what got you smiling? You had a big smile on your face when I walked in. Wouldn't be about 'Dingo, would it?" She smirked as she questioned me.

I thought about if I should share with Jamika the feelings I began having toward Trent, but I decided against it… for now at least.

"Girl, no. Please, nobody's thinking 'bout that nigga," I said, brushing her off.

"I was just thinking about something Miguel told me this morning." Her eyebrow shot up as if she didn't believe a word I just uttered, but she didn't say anything, and for that, I was grateful.

"What do you mean, you can't come pick me up, Miguel?" I whined into my cellphone as I paced the floor of my classroom. I looked at Heaven-Leigh as she sat there, oblivious of my plight as she colored away in her coloring book. Her mom was late picking her up. She was the only one here, and class was over fifteen minutes ago.

"Babe, my client switched up her time on me last minute. I have to work late again." Miguel was annoying the hell out of me at this very minute.

"Miguel, what am I supposed to do? You took my car back to the dealership for the remainder of the week, or had you forgotten?" I stomped my feet like the spoiled princess I was.

"Baby, please don't be upset with me. Just call an Uber this one time. I got you for rest of the we—" Before he could finish his stupid sentence, I hung up my phone on his ass.

"Stupid," I grumbled to myself softly as Heaven looked up at me then looked at the door.

"Is my mommy coming soon?" she questioned as she bent her head and resumed her coloring, which, by the way, was all types of awful but in a cute four-year-old way.

Going through my contacts, I found Heaven's mother's number and called a total of four times but got no response. Sighing heavily, I knew the next person I had to call to come get Heaven. I dialed his number.

"Destiny?" I closed my eyes at the sound of my name rolling off his tongue. It sounded like honey. Getting my feelings in check, I continued to let him know why I called.

"Um, your sister never came for Heaven. I tried calling her phone, but I got no response. She never picked her up."

Trent let out a string of curse words before finally letting me know he'd be there in a couple of minutes. Disconnecting the call, I walked over to Heaven and sat with her as we waited for her uncle to arrive.

"Miss Charles, do you like my uncle Trent?"

My eyes damn near bugged out my head at what she asked me. "Um, well… I like all my students' parents and relatives, Heaven." This was the safest reply I could come up with.

"I think you should be his girlfriend."

What in the hell? What kind of conversation was this for a four-year-old to be having? I smiled and shook my head. "Well, I'm sure your uncle Trent already has a girlfriend." I cursed myself for trying to get information about a man I had no business trying to stalk, especially when I was trying to gain that information from a toddler.

"No he doesn't."

I felt excited at what she revealed, and then I felt silly because, how could I take her words seriously? I touched the top of her head and smiled just as I heard the door open.

Turning to look at the entrance, Trent stood in the doorway, looking a bit flustered as he stared at his niece. As he stood there, I ate him up with my eyes. He wore a plain black T-shirt, a pair of gray sweatpants, and all-black Jordans on his feet. And let me say, when a man had that much meat between his legs, gray sweatpants should be banned. My body reacted instantly at just his presence.

"Yaay! Uncle Trent!" she shouted as she sprang to her feet. She really did love her uncle. I had to admire that. Grabbing up her belongings, I grabbed her hand and led her over to her uncle.

"I'm about to dig another asshole out of Tricia's neglectful ass," he mumbled as he took the stuff out of my hand.

I didn't say anything, because I was too nervous to strike up a conversation with him in case he asked what about Miguel and I, I walked away and began dialing up the number for an Uber.

"I didn't see your vehicle parked out front." I didn't bother to turn to face him as I answered.

"Mig—" I started to say, but then better sense prevailed. "Um, it's at the dealership. I'll have it back by the end of the week." I turned finally to look at him, and his eyes were traveling up my body as if I was standing there, butt ass naked.

"How you about to get home?"

"I was just about to call an Uber. I was just waiting for you to show up to get Heaven," I said as I put the phone against my ear.

"C'mon, let's go, I'll take you home." Those words casually passed his lips, but in my mind, all I heard was a voice screaming, *'Don't do it, Destiny!'*

"It's OK. I don't wanna put you out of your way." I shook my head at him. He walked over to me, his eyes never leaving mine, and he reached for my hand and took the phone away from my face.

"What I just say? Get yo' shit and let's dip."

When I say this man is obnoxious! I thought to myself as he walked away, taking Heaven by her hand with my cellphone still in his possession as he marched out the door.

Realizing that I had no say in the matter, I grabbed my hand bag up and followed Trent and Heaven to his vehicle.

"The hell you mean, you fell asleep, Tricia!" So Trent had been yelling at his sister for what seemed to be forever, but it was really just about a couple of minutes now. "You are so irresponsible! What type of mother forgets to pick her child up from school?" I sat awkwardly in the front seat of his ride as he roared through his cell, and Heaven was actually drifting off to sleep in spite of Trent screaming his head off as he drove.

"Man, forget you, Tricia!" Something told me he wanted to use another word, but I guess he was keeping it G-rated for Heaven's sake.

About ten minutes later, he pulled up in front of a medium-sized house, which I assumed was his, in a relatively quiet neighborhood. Putting his car in park, he got out and took a sleeping Heaven out of the backseat. She was so cute.

"I'll be right back," he said as he walked briskly to the front door with a sleeping Heaven on his shoulder.

A couple minutes later, he came jogging back to his car with an angry scowl on his handsome face. Not bothering to say anything to me, he started his car and pulled out on to the street. After a few minutes, I realized he was not going the way he was supposed to, to take my ass home.

"Where are we going?" I looked over at him, and he took his sweet time before he replied.

"I was on my way to check something out at my work when you called. I'll have to take you with me before I drop you off at home."

"The auto shop?" I asked cautiously, fearing his answer.

"Nope, the club."

Ugh, I groaned to myself, wishing he could just take my ass home before he went over to Stallion City. I wanted so badly to protest, but I wanted to stay on his good side, seeing as he hadn't questioned me about Miguel not one time.

I decided to play it safe and keep my mouth shut.

CHAPTER NINE

Trent

Destiny was lucky I was mad as fuck with my sister and that bullshit stunt she pulled, or I would have been all up in her ass, asking about that lame ass boyfriend she had and if she kicked his ass to the curb as yet. As soon as I cooled down, though, I was getting in her ass.

Tricia, on the other hand, was lucky she was my motherfuckin' sister, or I swear on my life, I would have beat her ass! Talking about she fell asleep—what type of bullshit was that? Who fell asleep, knowing they had the responsibility to pick their child up from school. I didn't know how much longer I would be able to tolerate her irresponsible self in my crib.

Reaching the club, I pulled into the parking lot that had just two cars parked—the owner's and LaLa's. I forgot all about LaLa and just prayed she would keep her crazy ass chill as I prepared to walk in the club with Destiny.

"Come inside with me real quick," I said as I opened up my door and hopped out. Destiny looked skeptical as hell as she stared at me from behind her glasses as if she was scared or something.

"Aye, there will only be about two people in there. The club isn't even open for business yet. No need to look as if you about to shit in your pants. C'mon."

She rolled her eyes at me, and I swore the next time she did that shit, I would punish her ass how I saw it fit.

Pulling the handle, she opened the door and stepped out. I allowed her to lead the way a couple steps so that I could admire her ass bouncing in her navy-blue, knee-length dress she wore with a pair of red pumps. Damn.

Picking up my pace so I could reach the door so that I could open it for her, I stepped to the side, allowing her to get by me. As expected, the club was empty except for LaLa and her girlfriend, Tracey. LaLa was tidying up the tables when she suddenly looked up and saw me. She smiled seductively at me until her eyes set on Destiny, and that smile evaporated faster than a puddle of water on a sunny day.

"What's up, ladies?" I nodded my head in a friendly greeting at them. Tracey was cool, as always, but LaLa just glared at me as if she wanted to bite my head off.

"Come back here with me," I said as I gently took Destiny by her elbow, leading her to the locker room so I could grab my costume for the night. Destiny looked around curiously and sat on the only seat in the room—the same wooden bench I fucked both LaLa and Tracey on just a couple weeks prior. The same day I met Destiny's ass.

"Trent?" Destiny said my name as I opened the locker door after putting in the combination. I looked over at her.

"How did you end up working in a club? Honestly, you seem to be a very educated man, so why here?" She smiled at me as she crossed her legs, waiting for me to reply. I contemplated if I should be totally honest with her, then I said to myself, *fuck it.*

"I came from a really fucked up childhood. My father beat me and my sister every chance he got; my momma was no different." Grabbing what I came for, I closed the locker door and continued on with my lil' history story. "Anyway, I was about seventeen years old, still living with my parents, when my dad came home one night, drunk as hell. He went into my sister's room and started beating the shit out of her for no damn reason. Her bawling her lungs out woke me up. Not even thinking twice, I ran into her room to save her, beating the shit outta my father in the process. I didn't even wait for that nigga to put my ass out. I packed my shit and left." Stopping my story, I reached and pulled the T-Shirt I was wearing over my head, tossing it next to where Destiny sat. I looked as her eyes slowly traveled over my abs and chest. She eyed all of my tattoos in curiosity.

"Yo, so you just left your sister alone with your father?" She stammered a little, focusing her eyes on me once again. "How old was she then?"

Reaching for the waistband of my sweatpants, I began lowering them. I heard Destiny gasp.

"Trent, what are you doing?" Her eyes were wide with fright as if I was about to try and rape her ass or something.

"I'm about to try on my costume for tonight real quick. I got it yesterday, but I didn't have the time to make sure it fit," I said, letting the sweats fall around my ankles. Destiny's eyes grew big when she saw my monster laying against my thigh, my boxers barely able to contain him. I thought her eyes were about to pop out their sockets, and those shits would roll around on the floor like a pair of tennis balls. That shit was funny as hell.

"And to answer your question, no, I couldn't take her with me. Tricia was only eleven when I left. But... I warned my father, letting him know if he ever put his hands on her, I would come back and murder his ass with no regrets." I slipped my legs in the fireman costume I decided to wear tonight because I wanted to switch it up from the usual loin cloth I normally wore, and I slid my arms through the suspenders.

"So seeing that I left home and had to provide for myself, I began working as a dope boy. That didn't turn out too well, because I had a lot of anger inside. I would be beating nigga's asses on the blocks for the smallest shit. And if I wasn't beating their asses, I was shooting them motherfuckers. After a while, nobody wanted to give me any of their product to sell. Said I was too much of a hot head and would always have the police on my ass. I came across the auto shop where I'm at now kinda by accident, and I've been working there ever since... for the past two years."

"So how did you end up here? At Stallion City?" She eyed my costume with a slight crease in her forehead as if she was confused.

"Well, one day at the auto shop, this nigga came by to get his Lamborghini detailed, and he started looking me up and down. I thought that nigga was gay, and I was only waiting for him to get out of line so I could beat his ass. Then he casually told me that he owned Stallion City and asked if I ever thought about making some extra money. I actually wanted to open my very own auto shop but couldn't afford it. So after thinking about it, I showed up here, and Joseph—that's the owner of the club—he hired me." Destiny smiled at me as if now she had a better understanding of me.

"So you trying to open your own auto shop?" she questioned as she looked me up and down as if she wasn't feeling my choice of costume.

"Yup, I think after about six months, I should have enough, so I'll be able to quit both jobs, and I can finally work for myself. I already saw a spot to purchase; I just have to get more money for the down payment. And why the hell you over there looking at my costume with your face all scrunched up?" I looked down at what I was wearing, beginning to doubt my choice of clothing.

"It's just… If your stage name is 'Dingo, then why the hell are you dressed like a fireman?" I laughed at the way she said it. Her glasses moved as she knitted her eyebrows together.

"Because, Destiny, I do whatever the fuck I want." Changing back into my regular clothes, I hung the fireman outfit back into my locker. "Since you know a little bit more about me, let me ask you something I've always been wanting to ask."

She gave me a curious look as she waited for me to ask.

"How'd you get that scar on your forehead? Does your nigga hit you?" I swore if she said yes, I would find out exactly where he worked and what he looked like and kill his ass myself.

Instead, she looked sad, and her eyes got distant. "No. Miguel would never hit me. But for now, I'd rather not talk about it." Since it seemed like it really made her unhappy, I let it drop... for now at least.

"Come on, let's go," I said to her as I held my hand out to her, helping her stand to her feet. Not even putting much thought into it, I bent and kissed her gently on her lips and took pleasure in the way she responded to me.

"I don't usually be kissing females on their lips and shit, but lately, you've had me doing things I don't normally do." Not waiting for her to reply, I pulled her gently, and we made our way out the door we came in.

As soon as I walked out, I bumped right into somebody. It was LaLa. I could tell her silly, stupid self was probably standing there a while, snooping on my conversation.

"Damn, LaLa, back off a little. You all in my grill and shit." Turning her attention on Destiny, she mean mugged the hell out of her. Before I had to lay this bitch flat on her back, I pulled Destiny out toward the entrance, passing Tracey's fine ass on the way out. I gave her a small head nod and left the club.

"What was that about? LaLa your girlfriend or something?"

Hearing the jealousy in her voice and thinking it was cute as fuck, I threw my hands around her neck and hugged her close to me. "Nah, you're my only girlfriend, Destiny," I said, chuckling.

What Destiny didn't know was that I was about to question the hell out of her ass about this alleged nigga in her life. I knew she was purposely trying to keep my mind off of asking her, but I wasn't a dumb ass... I knew what she was up to.

CHAPTER TEN

LaLa

I knew Trent didn't walk up in here with some random hoe!

My insides were on fire as I stared behind him and this nerdy-looking bitch with glasses on her face. He even had the nerve to not acknowledge me as he walked on by, like he was the king of this motherfucker. I didn't take too kindly to being ignored, especially by the only person I was presently fucking.

Let me break it down for y'all real quick. When Trent started working at the club about four months ago, I swore on everything, I fell in love with his sexy ass on first sight.

He had a nice Nutella color, all his sexy ass tattoos on his arms and chest, his nose rings, and his sexy ass physique. Mmmm, my pussy creamed every time he crossed my mind. I immediately started showing interest in him, but he let me know he wouldn't fuck anybody he worked with. He said that shit could get messy real fast.

But I needed his dick in my life. When I saw what he was working with, I just knew I had to have it. I mean, a bitch had her fair share of niggas; I wasn't gon' lie. But I needed and wanted desperately to have

Trent's dick slamming into my walls.

So desperate times called for desperate measures, and I made him an offer he couldn't refuse. One time when he finished his performance, I told Tracey, my girlfriend of about three months, to meet me in the locker room. Of course, it was the men's locker room, and we really weren't supposed to be in there, but I had a plan, and it had to be executed in that very room. When Trent came off stage, he 'accidentally' walked in on Tracey giving me a good tongue lashing. And being a man, he couldn't resist. When we made eye contact, I asked him if he would like to join us.

Ever since then, the three of us would hook up and have some good ass threesomes. However, I made sure to let Trent and Tracey know that the only way it would ever go down was between the three of us. They were not allowed to fuck one another without me being present. The reason why I came up with that arrangement was because I saw the way Trent looked when his dick was all up in Tracey's guts. He always looked as if he was enjoying fucking her way more than he enjoyed blowing my back out, and I just could not have that happening. If I ever found out Tracey was fucking my man behind my back, all hell would most definitely break loose.

Anyway, back to this random hoe Trent came with. So Trent just casually walked past me, taking little miss sunshine back to the locker room with him. Knowing that Trent stayed on his hoe shit, I followed them because I was certain he was about to run his long ass pipe up inside of her.

It turned out they were talking, like having a normal fucking conversation, something he never did with me. I stood there, eavesdropping from behind the door as he shared intimate details of his life with her. He never did that shit with me! What made this slut so special?

Adding insult to injury, he kissed her! This nigga was talking 'bout *he don't usually be kissing females on their lips.* He told no lies there. I'd been trying to get him to do just that to me, but to no avail. I was so deep into my stalking shit that I didn't even realize they were coming out the door until they bumped straight into my sneaky ass.

Realizing I needed to let off some steam before the club opened for the night, I looked over my shoulder at my girlfriend, Tracey, as she sat by the bar on her phone. Licking my lips, I called out to her.

"Tracey! Come here, baby." I smiled sweetly at her as she got up and made her way over to me. Tracey was always so willing. She was always ready to do anything you asked of her. She was my first lesbian relationship, and she for damn sure would be my last! I needed dick in my life; I couldn't even front.

She sashayed her fine ass over to me, wearing a short ass dress that barely covered her juicy, thick caramel thighs and ass.

Unlike me, Tracey was strictly into girls. She fucked Trent only because I told her to, and she knew it would make happy.

"Come eat my pussy. I'm stressed the fuck out." I grabbed her roughly behind her neck and pulled her face to mine so that I could kiss her.

Leading her to the bathroom where she, Trent, and I had countless sexual encounters in before, I pulled my skirt up as she got on her knees to service me.

If that lil' nerdy bitch thought I was just about to sit back and let her steal Trent from up under me, she had another thing coming!

CHAPTER ELEVEN

Destiny

I didn't even know why I was over here trippin', but I was anyway. I knew there was more to that LaLa chick than Trent was admitting to. She couldn't keep her eyes off me as if I stole something from her... or rather someone.

As those thoughts entered my mind, I turned to look over at Trent as he concentrated on driving. This nigga thought he was slick.

"I hope you're looking at me because you about to tell me you dumped yo' nigga."

Shit! I immediately looked away. I thought my plan to have him preoccupied with talking about himself would make him forget all about Miguel. I mean, what man didn't like talking about themselves?

"I'm not hearing you, Destiny." He turned for a brief second to look at me.

"You fucking LaLa?" I asked him, narrowing my eyes at him as I began to bite the inside of my cheek.

"Why you answering my question with another question that ain't got shit to do with the question I previously asked you, Destiny?"

The fuck? Is this riddle me this! This nigga was about to piss me all the way off, evading my question in a smart way.

"You answer me, then I'm gon' answer you." I rolled my neck at him. I didn't even know where all this attitude was coming from. This nigga wasn't mine, so I had no rights to be questioning him the way I was.

"No, I'm not fucking LaLa." This nigga was a whole liar.

I huffed at him as he turned onto my street. I was about to jump the fuck out of his car without answering his question and make a run for the door. I knew it sounded childish as fuck, but that was a personality he brought out of me.

Pulling my keys out my hand bag, he started slowing down as he came up to my house.

"So you not about to answer me, Destiny?" He looked mad as hell, but I could give a fuck.

"Kiss my ass, Trent. I saw the way that bitch looked at you, and there is more than you're saying. But you over here trying to get me to end things with a man I've been with for over a year. Whatever!" Pulling on the door handle, I jumped out of his car, walking as fast as my red pumps would allow me.

I heard Trent's car door open and shut, and he enabled his alarm. I wasn't even worried about him as I held my keys in my hand, making my way to the front door.

As I struggled to place the key in the keyhole, I felt his hard body press into mine.

"I don't know why you constantly think I'm playing with you, Destiny," he said with his lips pressed against my ear, his warm breath traveling along the back of my neck.

"Back up off me, Trent." I pushed my butt back, trying to get him to ease up off me.

"Open the door, Destiny." As if he found that I was taking too long, he roughly grabbed the key from my hand and shoved it into the lock, opening the door.

Pushing me inside of my own house, he slammed the door behind him as I stood with my arms folded as I glared angrily at him.

"Get out!" I said as I pointed at the door. Trent really had some nerve. I had a long day, and I was in no mood to be arguing with him right about now. I just didn't have the strength.

"Since it seems like you too chicken shit to end things with that nigga, I'm gon' make you want to leave him." I snorted loudly because I didn't know how he planned to do that.

Imitating the snorting noise I'd just made, Trent slowly began taking baby steps toward me as he continued to speak to me. "I don't even know the nigga like that, but I know he's lame as fuck, and he don't handle you right. Your body responds to me way easier than if you were getting the dick the way you supposed to." The distance between us was slowly closing in, and then I began walking but backward... away from Trent.

"When I had you against the door at your school, you were whimpering as I played with your pussy with the vibrator. Remember how you were rubbing up against my fingers, wanting more?"

I began feeling as if I couldn't breathe as I listened to him talk about our encounter. Trent kept walking toward me, and I kept walking away from him.

"Remember how fast you came when I put your pussy in my mouth? I wanna put your pussy in my mouth again."

I gasped as the back of my calves bumped into my sofa. I had nowhere else to go. Now as we faced each other, Trent smiled slowly as he licked his lips, his signature move that I loved to hate.

"Trent," I said breathlessly, unable to say anything else, unable to utter another word.

"Destiny, lift your dress up for me, baby." The sound of his voice was different, as it was now filled with lust.

I swore my brain was saying one thing, but my hands were betraying me as I began lifting my dress up over my thighs. Trent and I couldn't take our eyes off each other.

With my dress now up over my waist, Trent averted his eyes and looked at the black pair of lace underwear I had on.

"You already wet for me, Destiny?" His smiled broadened as he eyed the wet spot on my underwear. "Take those off." He pointed at my panties as he began rubbing his monster dick through his sweatpants. Removing my underwear, I was about to toss them on the ground when he said, "Give them to me."

The black lace in my hand, I placed in Trent's outstretched palm. Holding the material in his hand, he brought it up to his face and sniffed it, closing his eyes. I wasn't worried, because I know my stuff smelled good as hell.

Shoving my underwear in his pants pocket, he ordered me to sit at the end of the sofa with my ass halfway hanging off. "Open your legs... Wider."

I did what he said and felt totally exposed to him, but I didn't care. This shit was turning me the fuck on. Miguel would never do anything like this with me.

"Rub on your clit. Let me watch."

I was hesitant, very hesitant.

"Why you acting like you never played with your pussy before, Destiny? Pretty sure you got a vibrator under your pillow or some shit 'cause I know your nigga ain't getting the job done." I hated Trent right about now, and I hated that he was right about things like me having a vibrator and the sorry fact that Miguel sucked in bed.

Using my index and middle finger, I placed them between my legs and began rotating them against my wet, aching nub. Trent stood there, watching me as he bit into his lower lip, clearly enjoying the sight.

This shit felt so good. I dipped my head back and grinded my dripping slit against my fingers.

"Stop." I heard what he said, but I couldn't bring myself to stop. I knew the release I needed was close. "Destiny... stop." I felt his hand grab my wrist, and he pulled it away from between my thighs. I opened my eyes and gave him a look of frustration. Wasting no time, he got on his knees, putting his mouth on me, and I cried out in ecstasy.

"Tre-Trent," I was able to say, barely audible as he flicked his tongue mercilessly against my clit, his beard tickling the inside of my thighs. Grabbing my legs, he roughly pointed them to face the ceiling. Removing his face, he spoke to me. "You need a real nigga that knows how to handle this sweet pussy."

Using the tip of his tongue, he flicked it against my asshole, and I almost fell off the sofa.

"Aaahhhh!" I screamed out as I tried to run from his mouth, but he immediately tightened the grip he had on my legs.

"Stop fucking running, Destiny," he scolded me before putting his mouth back on me. He continued attacking my ass with his tongue while using his thumb to rub on my clit.

"Fuck!" I screamed out as my lower stomach began to feel heavy. I couldn't even remember the last time I used a curse word during sex. Unlike Miguel, I knew Trent wouldn't have had it any other way.

Feeling I was about to cum, I shut my eyes tightly as my clit got rock hard.

"Cum for me, Destiny. I know you about to. I can feel it," he said huskily, and I did. I grabbed on to his fade as I started gasping for air as if I couldn't breathe. Trent put his lips back on my pussy as he greedily sucked all of my juices as they ran out from me, making loud slurping noises in the process.

"You're so responsive to me, Destiny," he said as he kissed my mound as if he was in love with her before letting my legs go, putting them back on the floor. It was only then I realized I still had my pumps on my feet.

Trent got to his feet and stood directly in my face. The bulge in his sweats was big as fuck. I knew I would scream like a bitch, trying to take all of his dick in me. But I didn't care. I wanted to feel him inside of me.

Reaching for the waistband of his sweatpants, I began pulling them down, but he stopped me by placing his hand on mine.

"Nah, you ain't about to get this dick until you act right. End it with that nigga." *There he went again.*

I slapped his hand in frustration as he pulled his pants back up, and he just laughed at me.

"Just leave, Trent," I said as I got up and pulled my dress down over my thighs. He continued laughing at me as he walked over to the front door.

"I'll be your own personal chauffeur until you get your car back. I'll be here to get you in the mornings, then I'll be dropping your ass back home." I knew what Trent was trying to do. He was trying to keep me on a leash, making sure I had little contact with Miguel. Pulling my underwear from out his pocket, he placed it under his nose and sniffed it as he closed his eyes.

Smiling at me, he opened my front door and casually walked out as if he didn't just turn my world upside down. He slammed the door behind him as my chest heaved with rage.

I knew Trent was about to take me on a whole rollercoaster ride, and I was low-key looking forward to it.

CHAPTER TWELVE

Jamika

I stood on the scale at the gym and smiled. It had been about two weeks since I decided to change my eating habits and started exercising, and I had already dropped seven pounds.

I was feeling so different about myself. I was beginning to have more confidence, and Khalil didn't even bother me as much anymore. He was still doing his same old shit, coming and going whenever he felt. I was convinced more than ever that he was cheating on me with someone. One morning, he left our home in one color boxers, and by the evening time when he was changing to climb into bed, he was wearing a completely different pair.

Of course, I brought it up, and we ended up in full brawl. I'm talking 'bout hair pulling, fist to face, and all that shit. I ended up sleeping in my son's room. Khalil swore to me up and down that I was crazy and that he left home in the exact boxers he came home with, but I knew better.

I was about to call it a day at the gym. I was doing my warm down exercises when I noticed someone get on the treadmill next to the one

I was on. I glanced to my right and quickly looked away. Beginning to feel a bit nervous because this nigga right here that was next to me, running on that treadmill as if massa was running behind him to lynch his ass—this brother was fine as hell.

I'd noticed him the very first day I started at the gym. He was tall, buff as hell, and bald headed with a honey-brown complexion and a pair of piercing light-brown eyes. His body was clean of any tattoos except one that was on his neck—a pair of red lips. We always made eye contact, but that was it. We never actually spoke. It wasn't like he would be interested in someone like me anyway.

As the last five minutes of my time on the machine came winding down, I noticed tall and handsome next me was also slowing down. He was sweating like crazy after his energetic run.

"You look good."

Unsure if the voice that spoke was actually talking to me, I chose to ignore it.

"Hey," the voice said a little more persistently this time. I turned to look over at him, making sure not to miss a step because the last thing I needed was to fall flat on my ass, rolling off the treadmill in the process.

"M-me?" I stuttered as I pointed at myself. He smiled then, showing the most beautifully white, well-portioned teeth I'd ever seen in my life.

"Nah, the person behind you," he cracked as he shook his head. "You're new here, and I see you lost some weight... You look good." I didn't know if I should take his comment as a compliment or as an insult. So what was he really trying to say? That before I lost weight, I looked bad?

"Not that you didn't look good before—don't get me wrong—but you still look good either way."

Could this nigga read minds? It was like he read my thoughts and clarified his statement.

"Thank you," was the only reply I was able to think of. I felt like my brain had somehow slowed down or some shit. My machine beeped, letting me know my session was over, and I picked my water bottle up and prepared to leave.

As I was walking off, I felt a hand lightly touch my shoulder. I turned around, and he held his hand out to me. "My name is Eric. What's yours?" My stupid mouth wouldn't even open to give him a reply. Eric started looking at me as if I were some kind of mute.

"Jamika!" *Why in the hell did I just shout my name at him?* Good Lord, this was embarrassing as hell.

"Nice to meet you, Jamika." Oh shit, he had his hand out to me all this time, and I had yet to shake it. Mechanically, I raised my hand and shook his.

We stood in an awkward silence for a couple seconds, just kind of looking at each other.

"Your man is very lucky."

I knew he meant that in a good way, but I couldn't help but laugh.

"So he isn't lucky?" he asked me with a confused expression on his face.

"Let's just say he wouldn't think that he is."

"Then he don't deserve you," he said softly as his face grew very serious.

I swore my heart tightened in my chest by what he just said to me. "I have to go. It was nice meeting you, Eric." I turned to make my retreat, but he stopped me again, this time by placing his hand on my elbow.

"I'm sorry I keep tryna hold you back when you wanna leave, but can we exchange numbers? I would love to get to know you." I was floored. This fine specimen of a man was really interested in me?

"Um, OK, if you really want it." I was acting cool on the outside, but on the inside, I was screaming. Taking my phone out from the cellphone holder attached to arm, I took Eric's number, and he took mine.

"I'll be sure to keep in touch. It was nice finally getting to officially meet you, Jamika."

I smiled up at him, and he winked at me before we went our separate ways. I couldn't hold the smile that pulled at the corner of my lips... Stella was about to get her groove back, y'all.

CHAPTER THIRTEEN

Julissa

"Are you gonna leave me some money before you go this time?" Honestly, I didn't even know why I was still fucking with this obviously broke ass nigga. He was lame as hell, but he had some good dick, and he was fine as fuck. He kinda reminded me of the actor Michael B. Jordan.

Here we were, laid up in what was easily a four-star hotel. I just had my back blown out from one of my many niggas. He was getting dressed, ready to leave, but he needed to leave a little something with me first before making it through the door. Truthfully, I didn't really need his money, but I'd be damned if I would let a nigga get all up in my goodies for free.

"I gave you some money the last time we hooked up, Julissa." He stopped putting his jeans on to gawk at me.

"Pppfff! Nigga, a hundred dollars is hardly some money. Quit playing." I waved him off as I got out of the bed to get dressed myself. I had to hurry my unfaithful ass up and make it home to my nigga because he didn't play.

See, my man was what some may call a boss! He ran shit where we were from. He pushed crazy weight from marijuana to cocaine to counterfeit money. So when you had a nigga that ran the streets, guess what? He was hardly ever at home. Now don't get me wrong; even though I was doing crazy dirt behind his back, Shaun Phillips, known as Casper in the streets, would kill my ass dead if he ever found out I was cheating on him, bullet straight through the back of my head, I kid you not.

But what the fuck was I to do? Sit at home day after day, night after night, watching the fucking walls? Shaun told me I was never satisfied, but he was wrong; I would be satisfied if he would show me half the interest he showed in running the streets. I was tired, and I couldn't take the loneliness anymore, so I started doing my dirt behind his back.

I'd gotten so used to cheating that I didn't even feel bad anymore. Actually, I was surprised that I got away with it for as long as I did. I made sure that I was real careful, though. The niggas I messed with knew how to act their roles, and they knew their places. And their places were—they didn't fucking have one. Just run me some dick and some cash, and roll the fuck out.

"You never satisfied, I swear."

I looked over at his cheap ass and wrinkled my nose at him. "Shut the fuck up. You sound like my nigga."

Shaking his head, he smiled that boyish smile at me that always seemed to tug at my heart. If he weren't such a broke ass nigga, I would have considered giving him a chance. "When you gon' leave that nigga and get with me, on the real, Julissa."

I snorted at his question so hard my nostrils hurt. "Nigga, you got a whole family at home. Jamika would probably poison your ass if she found out you fucking her friend behind her back."

Blah, blah, blah, yes, I was fucking my friend's man... And?

Look, let me break it down for y'all. Jamika and I were cool and whatever. But seriously, how did Jamika really think she could keep a man like Khalil, looking like a fat ass! If Jamika lost about twenty pounds, I was sure she could probably keep Khalil at home. But nah, she was out here eating doughnuts and shit.

"I done told you I'm gonna leave her ass. Just say the word, and we can move in together, whatever you want to happen. You leave yo' nigga, and I'll leave Jamika's fat ass."

I sucked my teeth at him. Imagine me leaving a baller like Shaun to get with a broke ass—never gonna happen.

Furthermore, Shaun would kill both Khalil and me without so much of a second thought if I even played dumb and decided to leave him. "Yeah, sure, Khalil. I'll think about it." I rolled my eyes at his stupid self when he turned his back to continue getting dressed.

The only man that I'd allow to get my cookie for free, and I may even consider leaving Shaun for, was Trent. Oh my goodness! Talk about a fallen angel. Trent was everything I wanted in a man—sexy, handsome, and I knew he collected those coins. And don't get me started on that Mandingo dick he had between his legs.

I'd been trying to get with that nigga ever since the first day I saw him in the strip club. I may have given him over three thousand dollars easy for the past couple months I visited the club. I wanted to feel that big dick up in my stomach, doing damage to my internal organs, but he told me he didn't fuck his customers.

And then the other night, he approached to fulfill our little arrangement we had, and a bitch felt like she was on cloud nine. Things didn't really go as plan however, seeing that I never had a dick that big in my mouth before. But I planned to redeem myself real soon.

"OK, I'll leave first, as usual. Text me when you get home, alright," Khalil said as he bent and gave me a quick kiss on the lips. I watched him leave the room and shook my head with a sly smile on my lips.

If Jamika only knew her man was out here creepin'—with her friend nonetheless—that bitch would probably have an aneurysm.

CHAPTER FOURTEEN

Destiny

Trent had been wrecking my last nerves these past few days!

This nigga had been doing the most, showing up at my house every morning at exactly seven thirty. Heaven-Leigh would be sitting in the back, waiting patiently to tell me all that happened from the time she woke up 'til the time they pulled up outside my home. She was beginning to grow on me. She was such a precious and loving child. I saw why Trent loved her so much.

If him picking me up every morning and afternoon wasn't enough, if my phone so much as rang as I sat in his ride, he would grab it from out my hand and answer it! Who did petty, childish shit like that? I couldn't stand his ass.

Thank God that Miguel wasn't around for the past couple days, so I didn't need to worry about him popping up unexpectedly. Trent was still adamant that I needed to have zero interactions with Miguel. I had asked Trent time and time again why he thought I should leave Miguel, and even if I did leave, then what? What was going to happen between us then?

This fool didn't even have a straight answer for me, so why on earth would I go ahead and leave my man?

I had just enough of Trent's unstable ass, so today, I didn't even bother to go into work. When Trent showed up, blaring his horn outside my house, I came outside in my bathrobe, looking all sorts of terrible.

"What's wrong with you, Destiny?" He eyed me suspiciously, looking at me up and down.

"I don't know. I think I'm coming down with the flu or something." I gave a feeble cough, adding emphasis to my bold-face lie.

"Oooh, I bet it was Joshua that gave you the flu, Aunty Destiny," Heaven chimed in from the back seat, blaming one of my students in my class. I nodded my head in agreement, knowing damn well Joshua was innocent.

"I can't make it in today, Trent. Go on ahead and drop Heaven-Leigh off. I'm going back to bed."

Trent kept looking at me as if he was wondering whether to believe my lying ass. Eventually, he said he hoped I felt better, and he'd call me later on to see how I was feeling.

I walked back into the house and changed out of my robe and climbed back into bed. Truth be told, Miguel was bringing my car back from the dealership later on that afternoon. And there was no way in hell I was about to tell Trent that he didn't need to get me that afternoon from school, and my boyfriend was dropping my vehicle off. Trent was all sorts of petty, so no telling what he would have done had I told him that.

I made sure to call Miguel, letting him know I was at home, and he could drop the car off at my place. I laid my ass back on the bed, picked up my remote, and prepared to chill for the rest of the day... Trent-free!

"Let's go to the mall or something."

I raised my eyebrows at Miguel as we sat on the sofa, being our usual boring selves, eating a box of Chinese food he brought along with him when he returned my car to me. "Since when you wanna go to the mall, Miguel?" I asked curiously as I took a small bite of my food. My mind was distant as fuck because Trent kept calling my ass, but I never answered him not one time today.

Trent had my feelings and emotions all over the place. First off, did I really want to risk my relationship with Miguel to be with a stripper? I mean, yeah, he had a regular job during the day, and I got that he was just doing this whole stripping thing to acquire funds to help him open his own auto shop. But I knew the risks with being involved with somebody like Trent, and the number one issue would be women.

I knew how women got down; they were messy as hell. And Trent, walking around with all that meat in his boxers, would make matters even worse.

Looking over at Miguel, who was waiting for my reply, I checked the time on my phone and knew that Trent would have picked Heaven up from school by now. As I was about to put the phone down, a WhatsApp message came through. Already knowing who it was from, I opened it up.

I've been calling your ass all day, and not one time you picked up. I'm starting to think you played me with that whole you're not well bullshit, so I'm on my way over.

My eyes grew wide after reading Trent's message. I suddenly sprang to my feet as if my ass were on fire.

"You know what? I think a trip to the mall would be fine. Let me grab a quick shower, and we can leave." I ran in the direction of the bathroom so fast I almost fell over twice. When I was done, I went through my closet, choosing to wear a short, strapless denim dress. I didn't particularly like this dress, because my ass was too big, and the dress always rode up on my thighs. But I had no extra time to search for something else.

Timing myself, I got dressed in a record-breaking ten minutes, not even bothering to put a bit of makeup on my face. And I kept my hair down, not even running a brush through it. I popped my contacts in my eyes and headed to the living room.

"Come on. Let's go." I smiled sweetly at a shocked-looking Miguel as I walked over to the front door.

"I don't think I've ever seen you get dressed so fast, Destiny," Miguel said as he chuckled a bit, getting up from the sofa.

Man, let me say this; I opened that front door and walked out as if I were being held hostage with a gunman at my back! My steps were cautious as fuck as I kept looking from right to left, fearing Trent's crazy ass would pop out of nowhere.

As I sat in the front seat of Miguel's Porsche, I exhaled a sigh of relief. But I knew there would be hell to pay when Trent discovered that my car was parked in my driveway, but I wasn't at home.

After walking the entire mall for about thirty minutes, listening to Miguel talk about himself the whole time, I was just about ready to leave. I looked at my phone, and Trent hadn't tried calling me back. I didn't even know whether to be worried or relieved.

"Let's go get some ice-cream," Miguel said, not even waiting for me to answer as he grabbed a hold of my hand and dragged me in the direction of the ice cream shop. I groaned to myself because I'd had enough of this day and just wanted to get home.

As we sat around the table in the quiet ice-cream shop, I was trying my best to stay focused on Miguel's latest story about his client, while eating my vanilla ice-cream when I felt someone's eyes on me. Looking up, ice cream almost came spewing out my nose when my and Trent's eyes clashed with each other's… His eyes seemed as if lava was running out of them. He was looking mad as hell. He was standing at the counter, waiting to place his order. I was so busy staring at him that I hadn't even noticed he wasn't alone. He was with the chick that was in the club the day he took me there—not the LaLa chick but the other one.

After we had a staring match for about ten seconds, he began rubbing his beard, a sign I started to understand meant he was in deep thought. He smiled at me, but I didn't return the gesture. He turned to the female he was with and told her something. She looked my way, and the next thing I knew, he was coming over to where I sat.

Oh shit! This can't be fucking happening right now, I thought to myself as he got closer to our table. Miguel was oblivious to what was about to unfold. He was busy eating his cone as he looked through his

Instagram as he kept up with his chatter.

Bending my head, I said a quick prayer, asking God to not let Trent be on any type of fuck shit.

"Miss Charles? I thought that was you," Trent said as I was forced to look up at him. Trying my best to keep it cool and not lose my shit, I gave Trent a weak smile. My eyes traveled over his casual attire, a pair of light-blue sweat pants that hung below his ass, which showed off his sexy, toned physique, a matching blue t-shirt, and a pair of Nike slides on his feet.

"Hi, umm... Trent, right?" I said, pretending to not remember his name as I smirked up at him. Miguel began clearing his throat, and I realized he wanted to be introduced.

"Trent, this is... Miguel." I didn't have the balls to introduce him as my boyfriend.

"Miguel... the boyfriend, right?" Trent began rubbing his beard again, never taking his eyes off me as Miguel said yes.

Shaking his head, Trent continued on, "I didn't see you at school today. Are you sick, Miss Charles?" he asked, challenging me with his eyes.

"I was. I'm all better now. Your girlfriend seems impatient. Maybe you shouldn't keep her waiting," I implied rudely as I curled my upper lip at him as we continued to give each other a staring showdown.

I felt Miguel's eyes on me, but then his phone began ringing.

"I have to take this outside. Excuse me."

Shit! I screamed in my head as Trent began biting into his lower lip.

I definitely wasn't about to sit here and deal with Trent's bullshit, so I got up, pulling my dress down to cover my exposed thighs, and made my way over to the ladies' restroom, brushing past Trent. Thank goodness the restrooms were out of the eyesight of customers.

I closed the door of the single restroom, not even bothering to lock it. Big mistake.

The door suddenly pushed open, and Trent walked in as I looked up at him in shock. He closed the door and made sure to lock it behind him.

"The fuck is the matter with you?" I asked through clenched teeth as he stood glaring at me. "Are you crazy? Get out of here before we get caught." I walked up to him and pushed him in his chest.

Grabbing my wrist, he pulled me against him in anger.

"I called you all day, Destiny, and you never even bothered to pick up the motherfuckin' phone, not one time." His jaw clenched, and his nostrils flared, his mean mug on full one hundred.

"Get the fuck out of my way, and let go of my wrists." I struggled to free myself from his grasp, but he just held on even tighter. "Go back to your little girlfriend, Trent. Don't think I don't recognize that's the trick from the club you work at. You fucking her too?" I whispered harshly, feeling like a fool after the words passed my lips because I sounded like some sort of jealous girlfriend.

"Do you know how stupid you sound right now? What? You think I just fuck everybody? And for your information, she's gay. I came to get ice-cream for Heaven-Leigh since your dumb ass wanted to play games all day by not answering your phone, and I accidentally bumped into Tracey." I didn't even know if I should've even believed his lunatic ass right about now.

"And what you doing with that nigga? What I tell your ass? You spent all day with him, Destiny? Is that why you didn't answer any of my calls?" I narrowed my eyes at him because clearly, Trent was on some type of meds that I didn't know about.

"Let me go." I breathed heavily as he refused to let go of the death grip he had on my wrists.

Leaning into me, his eyes filled with rage. "You fucked that nigga today?"

Naw, I was done playing with Trent. I wasn't even about to answer that ridiculous question. So I stood there, staring at him with mad attitude.

Without warning, Trent suddenly spun me around and slammed my back against the door.

"Do you know how absolutely crazy this is right now, Trent? You asking me if I had sex with my own man?" I clenched my teeth as I spoke.

"Answer me then."

"No, I didn't. You happy now?" Narrowing his eyes a bit, he removed one of his hands that bound my wrist so he could inch it down my thigh to the hem of my dress. Slowly, he began lifting my dress up, and without any warning, he dropped to his knees between my thighs. Shifting my underwear roughly to one side, he put his nose straight on me!

"Trent! You're a fucking madman! The fuck are you doing? Get up." I was trying my best not to lose my shit as he took one long sniff of my pussy then stood up.

With a stupid smirk on his face, he said, "You lucky you didn't fuck."

These childish games had me mad as hell. "Fuck you, Trent." My chest heaved with rage. What grown man dropped to his knees to smell a woman's pussy?

The smirk on his face disappeared, and I instantly regretted having a smart ass mouth as Trent closed the space between us.

"What you just say?" He looked at me as if daring me to repeat what I just said.

But guess what? I wasn't ever scared.

"Fuck… you." I separated the words as I twisted my neck at him.

"Fuck me, Destiny?" He grabbed my wrists again with one hand and pressed me even harder against the bathroom door.

"Yeah, fuck you, Trent." I knew this sounded weird as fuck, but my pussy began to throb, my nipples grew hard, and my clit pulsed between my legs. This could not be possibly turning me on right now.

"Say that shit again, Destiny." He pushed his hand up my dress and ripped my underwear off. I gasped as he tossed the material to the floor.

"Fuck you, Trent." I closed my eyes as his middle finger touched my clit and rubbed on it slowly. My breathing was low and short as Trent circled my clit.

Using the tip of his tongue, he flicked it lightly against my lower lip. Putting his mouth against my ear, he whispered softly, "You ever fucked a stripper before?"

"Mmmm…" was my only response as the circles he made started moving faster. Lifting my leg and holding it in the crook of his arm, he finally released my wrists so he could reach the inside of his shorts to pull his dick out. I placed my hands around his neck for balance.

My eyes bulged at the size of him because I knew I couldn't possibly take all of Trent's length and girth. I started shaking my head as if I were having a seizure.

"Don't get scared now, Destiny, after talking all that shit. *Fuck you, Trent*," he said, imitating my voice. I gasped as I felt the tip of his dick at my opening, and just the tip alone had me nervous as hell.

"I told you I'll make you want to leave that nigga."

"No, I ca-I can't take it all." I put my hand on his waist, trying to ease him off me, but he slapped my hand away.

Putting his hand against my throat, he bit into his lower lip as he continued to enter me. My walls were being stretched to kingdom come. I opened my mouth, but no sound came out.

"Say *fuck me, Trent*," he whispered against my lips as he pecked my lips.

"Uughhhh." I groaned as his dick was now only halfway inside me. His movements were gentle as he rocked slowly inside of me as he tried to allow the rest of his length to fill me up.

"Say it." He applied pressure to my throat.

"Fuck me, Trent." I was able to get the words out. I was trying my best not to cry out with pain. Oh, but that pain was mixed with pleasure. I licked my lips as I watched the love faces Trent made. This was some real thot shit, fucking in a restroom at an ice-cream shop. I was going straight to hell.

Removing his hand from around my neck, he covered my mouth as I looked at him, perplexed. "It's my pleasure to fuck you, Destiny."

Oh, I knew what he was about to do, but it was too late. Gripping my elevated leg tighter, Trent pushed the remainder of his length inside of me.

"Mmmmpphhh!" I screamed against his hand that covered my mouth.

"Relax, baby. Just relax your walls, and the pain will lessen." I felt tears burning the backs of my eyeballs, and my body struggled to adjust to Trent's width and length.

I swore on everything, it felt like I was about to pass out. But when Trent began doing long strokes, in and out of me, I began to forget about the pain and thought about the pleasure his dick was giving me. I moaned seductively against his hand as he began playing with my clit.

"Fuck, Destiny, I love this pussy. That nigga never gon' get this pussy again. You hear me?" He placed his hand around my throat again and squeezed gently. I nodded my head in agreement because, quite frankly, I would have agreed to anything this nigga said to me right about now.

"Talk dirty to me. I know you got some freak in you. Let it come out." Trent and I were breathing erratically as we made a soft banging sound as we fucked with my back to the door.

It had been a while since I'd let that freak side of me come out while getting some dick, but I fell into character real quick. "Fuck this pussy with that big motherfucker. You wanted it all the time. Fuck it like you mad at it." I licked my lips as we held each other's gaze.

The way Trent smiled at me as I said that shit made him look evil as fuck.

Oh shit! I thought to myself.

Tucking his bottom lip between his teeth, Trent dealt with my pussy like a pure savage. He delivered deep, hard, long strokes as he continued rubbing my clit. I started moaning so loud he had to cover my mouth once again. I felt the buildup in the pit of stomach, knowing my orgasm was close.

"I feel it. Cum for me, Destiny."

And I did. My body convulsed as I came. Shutting my eyes tightly, I buried my face in the side of Trent's neck.

Pulling out of me, Trent got on his knees and placed one, single kiss on my pussy lips. Then he put his mouth on either side of my panty line and sucked hard. His unstable ass was branding me with hickeys on the sides of my pussy.

After he was done, he resumed the same position he had me in before. His strokes sped up, letting me know he was about to climax.

"Shit, Destiny, I'm sorry, but a nigga 'bout to bust in you." Like I said, this was some thot shit. "Aaahhhh." Trent groaned in my ear as he released inside of me. My hands were still wrapped around his neck, my face buried in the side of neck. We both breathed heavily as we tried to come down from our high.

"Shit, I apologize, Destiny. I didn't mean to not strap up and release inside of you. I'm disease-free, though. No need to worry. You on birth control?" he questioned me as he placed me back on the ground.

Now this lunatic decided to ask these questions. I wrapped a huge wad of toilet paper around my hand and prepared to clean myself off.

"I can't get pregnant," I said firmly, and he stopped adjusting himself back into his basketball shorts and gawked at me.

"What you mean, you can't get pregnant?"

I bent and picked up my underwear off the floor. It was in shreds, and I'd have to walk back out of this restroom commando style. I tossed it in the trash.

"Look, I'm not about to have a conversation about my uterus in here." Pulling my dress down, I stopped and inspected the hickeys Trent placed between my legs. I didn't even know how I was about to face Miguel when I stepped out of this restroom. I shook my head, feeling embarrassed by my hoeish ways. Never in my life had I ever done anything this reckless, not even when I was in a relationship with Terror.

"Damn, let me see those love bites I left on the sides of your pussy lips." He reached for my dress, but I slapped his hand away. He laughed at me as he pulled his pants under his ass.

"Think this shit is funny? Stay the fuck away from me, Trent. Laugh at that. Fucking nutcase. Be sure you don't walk out right after me." He was still snickering at me like the juvenile he was as I opened the door and left out of the restroom.

Miguel was walking back inside the ice cream shop, now ending his phone call with a worried look on his face. Thank goodness we were returning to the table at the same time.

The Tracey chick was looking at me as if she knew exactly what just took place. Her eyes averted to the back of me as if she were looking for Trent.

"What's wrong?" I questioned him as he reached for me.

"That was my mother on the phone. My dad had a heart attack. I have to leave town for a while."

"Oh no, let's just leave now and go home." I needed to get out of this mall as fast as I could, not only to get away from Trent but also to get my butt in the shower. I reeked of Trent; I could literally smell him on me. I only hoped that Miguel didn't notice anything, especially seeing that I felt as if I could barely walk properly. My pussy was pulsing like crazy. It felt bruised very badly.

I needed to soak in my bathtub, hoping that would ease the pain I felt.

As Miguel and I left the ice-cream shop, knowing I shouldn't have, I looked back, and Trent was walking toward the counter where Tracey stood. He looked up at me and smiled then moved his lips in a kiss gesture. I immediately turned around.

Trent was just a fucking asshole, I thought to myself. But he was an asshole with some good dick that had me doing exactly what he said—wanting to leave my man.

CHAPTER FIFTEEN

Jamika

"You ready?"

I looked over at Eric and smiled. "I'm ready. You scared?" I teased him, and we both laughed.

"Girl, who you talking too? Let's do this." Eric had now been my official gym partner since he introduced himself to me almost three weeks ago. He was the best. He would motivate and push me, never making me feel bad or putting me down. He was pretty awesome.

I'd never spent any time with him outside of the gym, though. There were eyes everywhere, and I knew if the wrong person saw me, they would go back and let Khalil know that I was creepin'.

Today, Eric and I were on the treadmill, and we were prepared to run for an entire ten minutes without stopping. Even though I knew he could easily do it, he made me feel as if I actually had a chance of winning.

"Let's do this," he said as we began running. I paced myself like he taught me and remembered exactly how I should be breathing as I ran at a good pace that I could manage.

Eric Phillips was the type of man any woman would be grateful to have in her life. He worked as a manager at one of the local banks where we lived, for over three years. And get this; this twenty-eight-year-old Black brother had no kids.

Can you imagine that? No kids?

He was single after he ended things with his girlfriend of five years after he went to her house unexpected and caught his best friend's dick in her mouth. We got to know each other so well over these past few weeks. We shared just about everything with each other.

I told him I was in a relationship with a man who obviously didn't love me anymore and that he was verbally abusive. He sympathized with me and told me I should have the courage to leave Khalil.

I didn't need anyone telling me that I should end my relationship with Khalil, because I knew that for myself. The thing about it was, I'd known Khalil my entire life, and I didn't even know what it would be like to move on without him.

My chest started burning, and I looked at the time displayed on the machine, and I had only three minutes left, but I felt as if I wasn't going to make it. Beads of sweat were running down my face, and my chest and back were wet. I glanced at Eric, and he looked as if he could run another thirty minutes.

"I think I'm gonna stop, Eric," I said breathlessly as I fought to make my final three minutes.

"You sure? You have less than two minutes left. Try to push yourself a little more."

I shut my eyes as sweat dripped into them, clouding my vision.

In the background, a familiar sound came through the speakers on the gym. It was Migos, Cardi B, and Nicki Minaj's "Motorsport." I swore that song gave me life and the extra push I needed.

"Eric, this is my song... What!" I clowned as I started singing along with the lyrics.

"Well get it then, lil' mama."

I laughed at him because Eric didn't have a hood bone in his body. He rarely cursed, and he didn't even use the words nigga or bitch.

I finished the rest of my run easily as the timer beeped, and the treadmill slowly came to a stop.

"I'm proud of you," Eric said as he came and stood next to me. He raised his hand so that I could high-five him. I laughed as I reached for the towel and began wiping my sweat off. Taking the towel from me, he gently wiped my face as we looked deeply into each other's eyes.

We smiled shyly at each other. "Can I ask you something, Jamika?" he asked as he placed my towel around my neck.

"Sure, Eric, what's up?"

He began looking nervous as if he wasn't sure he should ask what he was wanting to. "Um, there's this get together at work. It's nothing big. One of my coworkers got this big promotion..."

I gushed as I stood there, looking at this six-foot brother with muscles coming out of his eyes, nervous about asking me out.

"You asking me out, Eric?"

He looked at me and nodded his head as he began rubbing behind his neck. This was so cute, I thought to myself.

"I would love to," I said, and he cheesed hard at me then.

"OK, it's this Friday. I know your situation, so I can give you directions, and you can just meet me there."

I nodded my head in agreement. Grabbing ahold of my hand, he led me to the scale. We always weighed ourselves before we left the gym.

"Oh, wow, I lost three pounds." I was so proud of myself. No one could even know. I was keeping up with my training and my eating habits, and the results were showing. I'd lost a total of eleven pounds since I started, and it was beginning to show in my appearance.

My stomach looked smaller, my thighs looked a little slender, and they didn't even rub as much. I even caught Khalil checking me out the other day as I got dressed for work.

"I'm proud of you, Jamika, like really proud," Eric said as he embraced me. Part of my success was due to Eric. He never made me feel bad about myself and encouraged me on days when I felt the need to quit.

Both Eric and I left the gym, and he walked me to my car. As I climbed in, Eric bent and kissed me on my lips. It was just a light touch, but it felt awesome, and my pussy responded.

"I'll call you," was the last thing he said to me as I drove off.

I was on cloud nine. I collected my son from mom, who watched him for me so that I could hit the gym. He was sound asleep as I walked inside of my apartment and closed the door. I kissed his chubby cheeks as I gently laid him down in his crib.

As I stepped into my bedroom, I switched the lights on and almost had a heart attack. Khalil was sitting on the bed, fully dressed, as if he were waiting for me.

"Shit! Khalil, you scared the crap outta me. I wasn't expecting you to be at home," I said as I placed my hand on my chest. This nigga was sneaky as fuck sometimes.

"Where would I be at, Jamika? I do live here," he answered me with an attitude as if I were accusing him of something.

"Well, aight, Mr. Krabs," I joked as I began removing my clothes to climb in the shower. He stood up and approached me slowly. He was acting kind of weird, but I quickly brushed it off.

"Yo, where were you tonight, Jamika?" I wrinkled my eyebrows at him because, clearly, he couldn't be asking me that question when I was standing before him in full gym wear.

"What kind of question is that? You know I just came back from the gym."

He narrowed his eyes at me suspiciously, and I had to stop undressing to look at him. Something was up, but I didn't know what. But I for damn sure knew I was about to find out.

"Why, all of a sudden, you think you need to lose weight? Hitting the gym and shit, eating salads and fruit bowls."

My mouth was now open because, really? This nigga talked about my weight every chance he got, telling me I let myself go since having our son. He was barely even able to look in my direction when I got undressed, making me feel bad about my weight gain by comparing me to these fake, plastic bitches he saw on the television.

"Khalil, you've told me about my weight countless of times. Are you for real right now? And I'm not doing this for anyone but myself." I turned to walk away from him, but he grabbed me by my box braids and pulled me back.

"Ow! Khalil, what the fuck is wrong with you?" I screamed out in pain as he tightened the grip on my braids.

"Who's that nigga always up in your face when you working out? Huh? You fucking that nigga?"

Shit! I said in my head. How the hell did he find out about Eric? I was real careful to never meet Eric anywhere but at the gym, and no one at the gym knew me. At least I didn't think so. I didn't even confide in Destiny about meeting Eric. The only person I told was Julissa. And she wouldn't snitch, because she couldn't stand Khalil.

"I don't know what you talking about, Khalil."

He pulled my head back so roughly that my scalp was burning. If he kept this up, I was sure a few of my braids would come out in his hand. "Let me hear you keep entertaining that nigga, and I'll bust you in your shit!" He scowled angrily at me. Khalil rarely put his hands on me. There were two times in our entire relationship that he did so, and both times, he thought I was cheating on him.

This was another reason I had doubts about leaving Khalil. He suffered from Dr. Jekyll and Mr. Hyde syndrome. When he got really upset, there no telling what he would do.

He released me roughly, pushing my head forward, and I turned to look at him.

"You got some nerve, Khalil. You stay cheating on me with these two-dollar hoes. I'm nothing like you." I mean, I wasn't lying. Eric and I had never done anything other than talk. And then there was that brief kiss he gave me tonight, but that was it. Now, how Khalil found out about Eric, was the real question.

"Don't worry about what I'm doing. You lucky I don't stop your ass from working out, but I'm seeing the results. Don't make me drop your ass over some lame ass nigga." He mean mugged me before he turned and left our apartment.

Reaching for my scalp, I gently massaged it as I felt a headache coming on.

Stripping out of the rest of my gym attire, I walked quietly to the shower. As the warm water ran down my body, I started to consider if I should cancel my plans with Eric on Friday. If Khalil easily found out about meeting up with Eric at the gym, maybe he would even find out after we had our date.

After thinking about it for a few minutes, I decided I was going to go right ahead with my plans.

"Fuck Khalil," I grumbled as I lathered my body with my Bath & Body Works wash.

CHAPTER SIXTEEN

Trent

*D*estiny invaded every last one of my thoughts these past few days. And to be honest, I wasn't enjoying it one bit. I felt as if I had no type of control over my emotions. I wasn't the type of nigga that caught feelings over a female, so this shit with Destiny was new to a nigga.

I decided to go ahead and do what she said, and I left her alone. I told Tricia she had the responsibility of getting Heaven-Leigh to and from school. A little distance between Destiny and I was probably exactly what I needed. A nigga couldn't lie, though. Destiny had the type of pussy that would make a nigga get pussy whipped for real.

Her shit was tight, warm, wet, and sweet as fuck—a lethal combination. Not to mention, I climbed those walls without strapping up. I didn't even know how I could be so reckless, busting up in her, not bothering to pull out. The pussy was that off the chain. The next time I ran up inside those guts, I was making sure to strap up, though. Even though Destiny said she couldn't have kids, I wasn't about to take any chances.

"You don't hear me talking to you!" Tricia yelled at me, bringing me out of my thoughts.

"What!" I yelled right back at her big-headed ass.

Tricia rolled her eyes at me and exhaled loudly as if I annoyed her. "I said, Heaven and I are spending the night over at my friend Tasha's house."

I tilted my head at her because I was wondering if she was just saying that and if she was about to go over to the apartment of nigga that beat her ass.

"You sure that's where you taking my niece, and you not about to go over to that fu—lame nigga's apartment?" I stopped myself from saying fuck boy because Heaven would have pulled me up on it.

"What I just say, Trent? We going over to Tasha's." She gave me attitude as she twisted her neck.

"Aye, don't make me get in that ass. I'll bust your head open if I hear you took my niece back there." I pointed my finger at her, giving her a sinister look. She rolled her eyes at me.

"Heaven, you let Uncle Trent know if Mommy takes you back to Duane's apartment, OK?"

Heaven looked away from the television so she could nod her head at me. She was concentrating so hard on Peppa Pig, and I couldn't help but chuckle.

I turned to walk into my bedroom when Heaven suddenly remembered she had something to tell me.

"Oh, Uncle Trent, did you get Aunty Destiny a present?"

Not certain what she rambling on about, I shrugged my shoulders at her. "Why would I need to get her a present?" I raised my eyebrows quizzically.

"Because today is her birthday, silly."

I had to stop my jaw from dropping open. Today was Destiny's birthday? Nah, that couldn't be right.

"How you know, baby girl?" Heaven took a while to answer, as she was busy laughing at something Peppa said on the TV.

"Because Miss Jamika came over to our class and had us sing the birthday song for Aunty Destiny."

I scratched my beard thoughtfully. Never once had Destiny mentioned that her birthday was coming up. Females celebrated their birthday for a whole damn month. I wondered why Destiny didn't say shit.

Tricia looked over at me and smirked. Walking over in my direction, she whispered to me, "You ain't slick, nigga. You tryna fuck Heaven's teacher? You a straight up hoe."

I mushed her in her face, and she started laughing.

"Who said I'm still trying?" I stuck my tongue out at her and smiled.

"Eww, you're disgusting with your stripping ass."

I'd broken the news to Tricia that I started stripping a couple months ago. And she was cool with it. She even had the audacity to ask me to hook her up with one of the other strippers at the club.

"Man, shut up. What time you and Heaven leavin'?" Since I now knew that it was Destiny's birthday, I figured I was about to invite her ass over. My mind was already in overdrive on what exactly I could do to make sure I could have Destiny all to myself—mind and body... especially her body.

"In the next hour or so. You about to invite one of yo' jump offs over here?"

I sucked my teeth at her. Refusing to acknowledge her stupid ass question, I turned to make my way to my room.

"Aye, big head, I forgot to tell you. Guess who I saw about a month ago?"

I stopped and turned to look at her, not really interested in who she was talking 'bout because I didn't really fuck with many people; I preferred to keep to myself.

"Guess, nigga," she said, taking a seat next to Heaven in front of the television.

"Who, stupid?" I wasn't in any mood for any of these bullshit guessing games.

Rolling her eyes at me, which was one of the most annoying traits females had, I swear, she answered me.

"Your homegirl, Clarissa," she said, cheesing at me.

Oh shit! Clarissa? What the fuck was she doing back in town? Y'all remember Clarissa, right? The one I said was riding my dick when I was only thirteen years old? I never saw her again ever since she moved out of her parents' house when she turned eighteen, which had me wondering why she was back after all these years. I wondered how she looked. She probably still looked fine, and that pussy was probably doing more types of freaky shit now that she was older.

"How you even sure it was her? You were young when she left." Maybe Tricia was wrong and took someone else for Clarissa.

"Actually, she was the one who remembered me. She said my face hadn't changed a bit. She asked for your nasty ass too." Tricia smirked at me as if she knew something I didn't.

"Why you over there smiling at me?"

"Because don't think I don't know 'bout the both of y'all." She pointed her index finger at me and twirled it around, smiling like BoBo the Clown.

"Yo, you don't know a god damn thing." I was trying my best not to laugh because I knew damn well Tricia knew Clarissa and I were fucking. She caught us one time. Clarissa was on top of me, riding my dick like crazy. Our parents weren't home, and Tricia accidentally walked in on us. I lied and told her Clarissa was giving me CPR because I had fainted. Tricia was little, so I thought she would eventually forget about it, therefore never bringing it up again.

"I caught y'all, remember?" she said and burst out laughing. I shook my head and turned and walked into my room. The chances of me seeing Clarissa were slim, so I wasn't worried about what Tricia said. I was sure Clarissa was just visiting anyway, and eventually, she'd be on her way.

Standing in front of the mirror, I scanned my attire. My black sweatpants hung low under my ass, and a black wife beater hugged my naturally athletic upper body. Taking the Nike slides off my feet, I changed them for a pair of black and white Adidas sneakers.

I grabbed my phone off my bed and dialed the number of the one female that had me thinking about possibly not being a hoe in these streets to see what it would be like to fuck with one pussy every night. Just the thought of that made a nigga break out in beads of sweat.

"What do you want, Trent?" Damn, Destiny was always salty as fuck.

"Why you always barking at me? Damn." Just hearing her voice was enough to make my dick jump in my sweats.

"Didn't I tell you to stay away from me?"

"So why you answered your phone? On the first ring at that?" She stayed silent, and I smiled. *Yeah, that's what I thought; keep playing with me, Destiny.*

"How come you ain't never tell a nigga your birthday was coming up?" I grilled her as I began searching for my car keys.

"Because I don't celebrate my birthday. And besides, I don't have to tell you shit." Females were mean as hell when they were falling for a nigga and tryna fight that shit. I shook my head at Destiny's simple ass. She was easy to read.

"I'm coming to get your ass in the next three hours. Be ready." I didn't know what Destiny was talking about. Everybody needed to celebrate their birthday, so she was tripping, as always.

"Boy, I'm not about to go anywhere with you." Destiny always had something smart to say, I swore.

"Aye, I'll be there in the next three hours, and your lil' boyfriend better not be there, or I'm setting his car on fire," I told her as opened my bedroom door and stepped out.

"Kiss my a—" Not giving her time to curse my ass out, I hung up the phone on her angry ass.

As I made my way out of the house, I stopped and kissed Heaven and mushed Tricia's face before I left the house.

I had a nice lil' surprise planned for Destiny, but I had to go shopping first.

****

I honked my horn outside of Destiny's house the exact time I told I'd be there.

I waited for about five minutes. I was almost daring Destiny not to come outside so I could act a fool. But her ass knew better, and I smiled to myself as the front door opened, and she walked toward my ride.

I licked my lips like a thirsty dog, and my eyes were glued on her as she made her way to me. Destiny was definitely looking like a whole meal. She wore a black sweat suit with the word Pink written on the side and a pair of olive green Rihanna Fenty bowtie sneakers on her feet. Her hair was down and fell to her shoulders in tight, kinky curls. She wore little makeup with just a pink gloss on her full, pouty lips. And of course, her glasses sat firmly on her face. She had a green clutch in her hand, and she opened the door and quietly sat down, not even looking at me.

My plan for the evening was just to make Destiny feel a little bit special on her day. But if she kept up with her funky ass attitude, I would just drop her ass back over to her place and forget about it.

Ignoring her attitude, I reached across the seat and hugged her. "Happy birthday, shorty." I placed my hand under her chin and gently kissed her on her lips. She responded by opening her mouth up for me, and I stuck my tongue in.

Finally pulling away from her, I looked into her face, and she blushed and smiled at me.

"Oh, we smiling now," I teased her, and she playfully pushed my upper arm. Not wasting anymore time, I drove her off in the direction of my home.

My gentleman swag was on full one hundred when we pulled up to my home. I got out of the car and made my way over to her side and opened the door for her. She got out, and I saw her looking at what I had on. I'd changed from the sweat pants and wife beater I was wearing earlier. They were replaced with a pair of black joggers and a black sweater with a pair of black Prada sneakers.

"Why are you being so nice?" she cracked as we held hands, walking to my front door.

"Come on now. I can't be obnoxious every day." Letting go of her hand, I unlocked the door, feeling nervous all of a sudden because I'd never done anything like this for a female before.

I stepped to the side and allowed Destiny to walk in, and I heard her gasp as her eyes fell on the table I had laid out in the middle of my living room.

She turned to me and smiled as I closed the door. "You did all this for me?" She examined the display on the dining table. A bottle of Moët was chilling in a bucket of ice, and a bowl full of strawberries with melted chocolate to dip in at the side. A tall candle stood in the middle of the table, illuminating the room. A meal of Asian takeout was dished out, which I bought from a restaurant downtown because a nigga couldn't cook for shit.

"This is really nice, Trent." She looked at me incredulously. She reached for my hand and leaned into me. Standing on her tiptoes, she kissed my lips gently, and our eyes remained open as our lips touched.

"Thank you, Trent."

Operation: Get Destiny, was now a success; I thought to myself.

CHAPTER SEVENTEEN

Destiny

I hated my birthday!

Most people turned up for their birthdays, but not me. I just prayed the day would end as quickly as it could. This day brought back a lot of painful memories that I just didn't know how to deal with.

I knew Heaven-Leigh had to be the one to tell Trent it was my birthday, seeing that Jamika couldn't just leave it alone and came across to my classroom so that my kids could sing for me. She also wanted to take me out tonight, but I just wasn't feeling it. She, along with a few other people, knew what happened on my birthday almost six years ago—the reason why I hated it so much.

I tried my best not to lust after Trent as we ate our food. I did my best to stay away from him after our little run-in at the ice cream shop. There were times I thought about that day, and my knees got weak, and my clit pulsed in my underwear. Then there were days when I thought about it and felt like a hoe that I actually allowed Trent to fuck me in a public restroom.

My pussy pained me for four whole days after that incident. I was scared to pee; I was scared to wash myself properly while having a bath. Never in my life had I ever had to soak my pussy in Epsom salt to ease my pain and bruises. I was beginning to think my pussy would never be the same again.

"You still mad at me?" Trent asked, slowly chewing on his food as he looked at me. He was so fucking fine. I hated myself for letting him affect me the way he did. He smiled and licked his lips, and I felt a warmth between my legs. Dammit, pussy!

"No, I'm not mad, Trent." It was the truth. I couldn't stay mad at his big head, even if I tried to.

"Why you over there being all quiet?" he questioned me as he took a sip of his Moët.

"What do you really want from me, Trent?" I asked, looking across at him. I took the glass of Moët and sipped slowly as I waited for his reply.

Putting his fork down, he sat back in his seat and crossed his arms as he toyed with his beard. He licked his lips as he continued to study me. The room was deathly silent.

"I want you to stop fooling yourself. You don't care about the nigga you with." His words irritated me because he was right.

"How do you know?"

"Look around, Destiny! It's your birthday, and who are you with right now? I just know you don't want to be with him, which leads me to my next question... Why are you doing it? You and I both know you don't love that nigga."

124

I bent my head and cleared my throat. Trent saw straight through me, and we hadn't even known each other for long.

"Talk to me, Destiny. What's up, shawty?"

I looked at him and picked my glass up again. Drinking the glass of champagne in one gulp. I decided to be honest with Trent. He wanted the truth, so he was about to get it. And it wasn't going to be pretty.

"I killed my father." This fool started choking on his Moët. I had to jump up and go pat him on his back.

"What? You shot that nigga?" I mushed the back of his head as he got up from his chair and faced me.

"No, stupid."

Picking the bottle of Moët up, he took my hand and led me over to his sofa where we sat down. Drinking straight from the bottle, he handed it to me.

"Tell me what happened then."

Taking the bottle, I took it straight to head as I started reliving a part of my life that I didn't wish to remember. "There is a reason why I don't celebrate my birthday. My dad died on that day." I sighed softly as I remembered that day as if it were just yesterday.

My boyfriend at the time, Terror, told me he was taking me to a party to celebrate my seventeenth birthday. I knew my dad would have forbidden it, so I planned to sneak out of the house that night. My father was a single parent; my mother died shortly after I was born, having complications from the cesarean section she had to bring me into the world.

I had absolutely no recollection of her, of course, so I knew about her from stories my father told me about her and pictures he showed me.

My father did his best to bring me up the right way, but Terrance was just somebody I couldn't shake. We met one Saturday at a popular roller rink where we lived. I was with a few of my high-school friends, and Terrance was with a group of his friends. They were being loud and rowdy, causing trouble. I'd heard about Terrance from my friends, and I knew he was nothing but trouble. He approached me that day. He was tall and light skinned, nice chestnut eyes, and shoulder-length dreads. His left arm had a full tattoo sleeve, and he wore a big, iced-out gold chain around his neck. Terrance was a skinny motherfucker, but that didn't bother me at all.

He came up to me, talking all in my ear, letting me know I was the baddest bitch in the roller rink, and he wanted my number. I didn't hesitate to give him my digits. Terrance and I were inseparable after that. My father worked long hours at the local Walmart where we lived; he was a supervisor there. Because I had so much free time, it was easy for Terrance and me to hook up.

A month after meeting Terrance, he took my virginity in the back seat of his Cadillac. I was screaming and clawing at his chest, begging him to take it out because it was hurting so bad. A month after that, I was riding him and sucking his dick like my life depended on that shit.

My seventeenth birthday was approaching, and Terrance told me that one of his homeboys from the hood was throwing a house party. Knowing very well my father wouldn't permit me to go with Terrance, I lied, saying I caught a stomach virus that day, and I went to bed early.

Eleven o'clock that night, I snuck out of the house, knowing my dad was fast asleep.

I walked a few feet away from my house where Terrance was parked and got in the car with him. The house party he took me to was something straight out of the movie Project X! There was weed smoking and sex, and the music was loud as fuck. Somebody called the police and reported it. When the cops got there, everybody scattered, running and screaming. Niggas were jumping through windows just to avoid getting locked up. Terrance and I managed to escape through the back door, but as we were making a run for it, two officers caught us. They took us down to the police station.

I had no choice but to call my father at two in the morning to come get my ass from the station. He was mad as hell. He cursed Terrance out, telling him he was no good for me and that he was never to see me again. On our way home, however, we got into an accident. Some drunk driver ran the red light and ran into us. My father died on the spot. I woke up in the hospital, only to find out my father passed away. I felt guilty as hell to this very day. It was like if I hadn't been at that party, and he didn't have to leave the house to come get me, he would still be alive today.

"That's why you said you killed your father? Destiny, stop trippin'." Trent took my hand in his, and he gently rubbed my fingers.

"That wasn't your fault. You can't blame yourself." What Trent said, I'd heard more times than I could count, but I couldn't help the way I felt.

"When I met Miguel, I just knew if my father was still alive, he would have approved of him. He was everything Terrance wasn't. He was well spoken, he had a promising career in law, and he wasn't from the hood. So you're right. I don't love Miguel, not the way I should anyway, and it's wrong that I've been with him this past year, knowing I got with him for all the wrong reasons. I've never celebrated my birthday since the day my father died. It just don't ever feel right."

"Look, baby, you can't continue living your life to please somebody that's not even here. So starting from today, you'll be doing things differently. I got a few surprises for you." Trent got up and disappeared through a door and came back with a couple of gift bags in his hand. My head was buzzing from almost drinking the whole damn bottle of Moët.

Standing in front of me, Trent handed me the first bag, which was very small.

"You got me presents, Trent?" I looked up at him as I gushed, taking the bag out his hand. A wide smile was on my face as I took out the little gift box and opened it up slowly. Inside was a gold chain with a heart-shaped pendant that read *Destiny*.

I had planned on staying mad at Trent all night, but how could I have stayed angry at him when he was doing thoughtful shit like this?

"Oh my goodness, I love it, Trent. Thank you." I stood up so that I could wrap my arms around his neck. Turning me around, he put the chain around my neck and hooked it. Pushing me back down on the sofa, he held up another gift bag, but this one was a little bigger than the first.

"I'm glad you liked that one 'cause you gonna love this one." With an evil smile on his lips, he waited in anticipation as I opened up the bag. The contents at the bottom of the bag had me shoving the bag back into Trent's hand.

"Uh-uh, forget it, Trent. I'm not wearing that." I could literally feel my face turning red. In the bag was a pair of black lace underwear and a matching bra with a sheer black robe to throw over.

"Aye, let me treat you how I want to just for tonight. Go in my room and change. Let me put on a show for you."

I raised my eyebrows at him. "A show?"

His hand outstretched before me, and I reluctantly put my hand in his, and he pulled me up.

"Yes, a show. Now go change." Shoving me into his bedroom, he handed me the gift bag before he closed the door, giving me my privacy. Not even believing what I was about to encourage, I slowly undressed, replacing my clothes with the ones Trent bought for me. How Trent actually knew my exact size of clothing was a mystery, but I guess he had to be an expert in women's clothes sizes from all his years of being a hoe.

I stood before the mirror and examined my reflection. This was fucking crazy! I had a man that was out of town, tending to his sick father, yet here I was, being *Thoterella!*

Thank God for the Moët because that was what gave me the confidence that I needed.

There was a soft knock on the door. "Damn, Destiny, how long it take you to put on a damn thong?" He opened the door, and we stared at each other. Trent was now wearing his sinful gray sweatpants and nothing else, his body glistening as if he had rubbed himself down with baby oil. This nigga was about to be the death of me.

"Shid, you looking fine as fuck," he said as he made a circle around me, getting his eyeful.

"Why does this underwear have a pouch in the front of them?"

"Don't worry about all that. Let's go." Once again, he took my hand and led me out to the living room. There was now a single chair that stood in the middle of the room. Leading me to it, he gently coaxed me to sit by putting his hand on my shoulders.

"Don't worry. I'm not gonna do anything you won't love."

My skin burned in anticipation as Trent took three red bandanas out of his sweatpants pocket, leaving me to wonder what he was about to do with those.

Stooping so that he was at my feet, he tied each of my ankles with two of the bandanas, and my legs were now wide open. The robe wasn't tied, so my bra and lace panties were on full display.

"Why are you tying my feet?" I asked as I looked down at the top of his bent head.

"All you gotta do, Destiny, is sit back and relax. I got this." He winked at me as he got up. "You know that pouch in the underwear you were talking about? It's there for a purpose."

I tilted my head at him as he once again reached into his pocket. He held two black, palm-sized items in his hand. Closing the space between us, he reached between my legs. Taking one of the black items, he slipped it inside of the pouch in the underwear. I was completely confused.

"What is that?" I questioned him as he smiled wildly at me. He pointed the other black item at me, which I was now able to see was some type of small remote.

Trent said, "You wanna know what it is?" He pressed one of the buttons.

"Aahhhh." I moaned as I tilted my head.

Fuck me sideways, they were vibrating underwear. I immediately reached for the vibrating device he placed in the pouch of the underwear.

"The fuck you doing?" He slapped my hand roughly away, "See, now this is what the third bandana is for." I sat helplessly as he began to tie my wrists to the back of the chair. So I was now bound by both my feet and wrists, powerless to Trent for him to do as he pleased.

Standing, stroking his beard, drinking me in as I sat spread eagled before him, Trent bit into his lower lip. His eyes were filled with raw lust. I squirmed under his gaze. I wriggled my feet, and I pulled against the bondage around my wrist. This was some freaky shit, and I was completely turned the fuck on. My pussy pulsed and leaked in the vibrating panties. I was hoping my ass wasn't about to be shocked.

"You ready?" I didn't even have an answer for his ass. Trent walked over to his laptop that sat on top of the coffee table. He tapped on a button, and the room filled up with soft music.

I like it when you lose it,

I like it when you go there,

I like the way you use it...

Oh shit! This was my jam! The sweet voice of Tank could be heard through the speakers of the laptop. Taking his spot before me, Trent held a couple of strawberries in his hand with the bowl of melted chocolate in the other. Standing firmly between my thighs, Trent dipped a strawberry into the chocolate and held it up to my mouth, and chocolate dripped down on to my breasts.

"Open your mouth, Destiny."

With me looking up at him and him looking down at me, I did exactly what I was told, and Trent placed the chocolate-covered berry into my mouth. As I bit into it, our eyes never left each other's. As I chewed the fruit, Trent took another strawberry and dipped it into the chocolate. Putting it to his mouth, he devoured the entire fruit in one bite.

He bent and placed the bowl of chocolate at my feet. Standing up again, he dug in his pocket as he took the remote for the underwear out once again. I was prepared for it this time.

Smiling down at me, he swayed his hips to the beat of the music. Then he took his hand and ran it down his tattooed, oiled-up, muscled chest, looking sexy as hell as he did so.

No words were needed as Trent bent his head to mine and captured my lips with his. I opened my mouth in anticipation as our tongues entwined, and the sweet taste of strawberries and chocolate mixed with our saliva.

Removing his lips, he traced his mouth over my neck and down to my breasts where he hungrily lapped at the chocolate that spilled there.

"Mmmmmm..." I groaned as Trent pressed the remote for the

panties to start vibrating again. I was in a lust-filled heaven as Trent pulled on my bra, exposing my nipples. He greedily took one of the hardened nubs into his warm mouth.

Who came to make sweet love? Not me

Who came to kiss and hug? Not me

Who came to beat it up? Rocky

And don't use those hands to put up that gate and stop me.

Tank sang "When We" in the background as I grinded my hips in the chair against the underwear while Trent's tongue lapped and sucked at my nipples. With the tip of his tongue, Trent made a trail from my stomach to the outside of my panties. He playfully bit into my inner thigh as his eyes feasted on the way I wound my hips against the chair.

"Fuck, Destiny," he said as he cupped the underwear, keeping the vibrating device in one place. My clit throbbed and ached as I felt myself on the verge of exploding.

Turning the underwear off, Trent roughly shifted it to one side and wrapped his tongue around my clit.

I struggled against the restraints on my wrists and ankles as Trent's tongue circled, flicked, and lapped at my clit.

"Trent!" I gasped breathlessly as he took his finger and dipped it in the bowl of chocolate at my feet and rubbed the chocolate against my slit. Putting his mouth back on me, he sucked and licked every last bit of chocolate off my pussy.

"Rub that pussy in my face." Trent stuck his tongue out as I ground against his mouth, my orgasm seconds away. I dared not look away as he devoured my pussy. His eyes never left mine as his tongue sped up and flicked back and forth against my clit. I was going fucking insane.

"Ssssssss... Trent!" I gasped loudly as I bucked my hips as I came hard, my juices running out of me as he drank every drop.

Trent hurriedly undid my ankles and wrists. Grabbing me by my upper arm, he pulled me to my feet.

"You got on way too many fucking clothes." Stripping me with an urgency as if his life depended on it, he lifted my body, took me to his room, and laid me on his bed.

Taking a condom off his dresser, he tore it open as he dropped his sweatpants.

I lay there, saying a eulogy for my pussy that was about to be murdered. I couldn't take my eyes from off the length and girth of Trent's dick that was about to enter me.

Trent came walking to the bed, stroking his larger-than-life dick in his hands. My coward ass began backing up on the bed, but Trent grabbed me by my ankles.

"You ain't about to go nowhere. Fuck you thinking?" he growled at me as he dragged my ass back down to him. As he lowered himself on me, I started breathing as if I were hyperventilating.

"I ca-I can't take it all," I stuttered as I used my hand to block him from proceeding by putting my hand between us on to his waist.

"That's what you said the last time. Now move your fuckin' hands, Destiny," he said through clenched teeth as I felt him place his tip at my opening.

"Uughhh." I groaned as he pushed his way in. I felt my walls expanding, stretching to its limits as Trent pushed his ten inches slowly inside of me.

"Fuck, baby. Relax and let this pussy take me all in."

I tried my best to allow my walls to relax, making it easier for Trent to gain access. I bit into Trent's bicep, and my eyes squeezed shut as my body tried to accommodate his size. When he finally had all of him inside of me, he began moving, making long, deep strokes.

"Fuuuuuck, Destiny, I'm sorry… but I'm about to beat this tight pussy up, baby." Taking my legs, he bent them until my knees touched my chest. I reached over my head to grab a hold of the headboard because this position right here was about to fuck shit up.

I cried out Trent's name repeatedly as he drilled into me, stroke after stroke. His hips rocked back and forth, then he moved them in a circular motion. My hands gripped the shit out of the headboard as Trent did some serious damage to my insides. He licked and sucked the side of my neck as he pounded into me. The pain mixed with the pleasure was enough to make me feel as if I could literally pull all of my hair out.

"All mine, Destiny. This pussy is all mine, you heard me?" he whispered hoarsely inside my ear. As he grabbed a fistful of my hair, I moaned as I agreed with whatever the fuck he wanted to hear me say. This dick was fucking me into a whole other dimension.

All the while, I heard Tank singing in the distance…

When we… fuck. When we… fuck.

CHAPTER EIGHTEEN

Jamika

It was Friday, and I was a ball of nerves. I was eating my tuna sandwich and sipping on a bottled water with Destiny on our lunch break at school.

"You did what!" I was trying my best to keep up with all this tea Destiny was spilling about her and Trent. I didn't even know she had that kind of shit in her, yet here she was, cheating on Miguel with an exotic dancer.

"Bitch, in a public restroom? Get your life, Destiny." I laughed as she covered her eyes with her hand.

"So what about you and Miguel? Is it over?" I had no clue that Destiny and Miguel were possibly having issues, but one thing I knew for sure was that they somehow didn't fit together. I didn't know, but it just seemed as if the relationship was somehow forced, if that made any sense.

Destiny exhaled as she began rubbing her temples. "Jamika, I felt so horrible. I mean, he's dealing with so much—his dad being sick and all. Then my evil ass called him up and told him I didn't think it was working out between us."

"Damn, and what he say?" I knew I was being nosy as hell, but I planned to confess to Destiny about Eric as soon as we were done gossiping about her and Trent.

"As expected, he was confused. He told me he thought he made me happy, and I was just talking crazy, and when he gets back home, we'll sit and talk about it."

I chuckled because, clearly, Miguel was not getting it. "Girl, you gon' end up with a case of fatal attraction on your hands. Be careful," I warned her, but she shook her head. Destiny just didn't know just how crazy some men could get. They often didn't display those characteristics unless you decided to leave their asses. Then you'd see their true crazy side.

"So what now? You dating Trent or what?"

"Girl, I don't know what I'm doing, Jamika. All I know is that when I'm around him, he gets on my last nerve like 80 percent of the time. But when he's not around me, I can't wait to see his obnoxious, rude ass." She curled her lips in and smiled. This bitch was dickmatized, on the real.

"He gave it to you that good, huh?" We laughed again as she nodded her head yes.

"Anyway, I got a confession." I bit into my lower lip as I tried to suppress my smile as I thought about Eric. Her eyebrows shot up as she looked at me in curiosity. "I met someone." We both squealed in delight as she high-fived me.

"Jamika! Who? When? Give me the details, girl." Destiny was just as nosy as I was. I filled her in on Eric and meeting him at the gym and how he always encouraged and pushed me to meet my fitness goals.

"Really, Jamika, that's great, and you look wonderful. I'm so happy for you. Did you kick Khalil's ass out the house yet?" she asked, and I playfully shoved her upper arm.

"We're going out tonight," I whispered as if there were someone else in the room, and they could hear me. Destiny's eyes grew wide, and she opened her mouth just as wide. She looked like one of those cartoon characters.

"Bitchhhhh, you better not let Khalil catch you. You know how his temper can get," she fussed at me, but I wasn't worried about Khalil, at least not too much.

"That's the thing. He already knows I met somebody at the gym."

"What! How? Did you tell anybody else besides me?" she questioned me, and I confided in her that the only person I told was Julissa. "Ew, why you tell that hoe your business, Jamika? I done told you so many times about her. I don't trust her ass." Destiny took a sip of her Sunny Delight orange juice as she turned her nose up at me.

"You know Julissa and Khalil can't stand to be around each other, so I'm pretty sure she wasn't the one."

Destiny rolled her eyes at me dramatically. Destiny didn't like the best bone in Julissa's body from ever since I could remember. She really didn't have a solid reason; she just said she didn't like her, and that she seemed shady.

"Watch that girl, Jamika. Don't say I didn't tell your ass." We chatted it up for a few minutes before we had to return to class.

"So where you about to tell Khalil you're going tonight?" she asked as we walked down the corridor to our classrooms.

"I told him my mother started a book club, and she invited me to join."

Destiny fell out laughing. "Just don't forget to give me the 4-1-1. I'll see you later, girl."

We said our goodbyes and made our way to our classrooms.

****

"Ma, just in case Khalil calls you up and asks for me, cover for me, alright? I won't be too late." I stood in front of the mirror in my mother's bedroom as she played with my son. I wore a stretch, baby-blue romper with a pair of wedge heels, and my braids were styled in an updo. My makeup was light, and I had to hand it to myself; I looked cute as hell. My weight loss was showing in the outfit I wore.

"Jamika, don't you dare get me in you and Khalil's mess. What are you thinking?" My mother sucked her teeth at me. She didn't really care for Khalil, but she tolerated him because he was my man and the father of my son.

"C'mon, Ma, just cover for me is what I'm saying," I fussed as I turned to look at her, and she looked me up and down while shaking her head.

"Girl, get out my damn house and be back here before midnight. My man is coming over to climb my walls."

The fuck? I did not need to hear that.

"Ma, that was pretty gross what you just said. That's all I'm saying."

I turned my nose up at her, and she threw a pillow at me. I laughed as my phone began ringing. It was Eric.

"Hey, Eric." I put on the sweetest voice as I blushed like crazy.

"Hey, beautiful, I'm leaving home in a few. You ready?" His voice sounded so beautiful over the phone. I felt like I was on cloud nine, and all we ever did was talk.

"Yes, I'm walking out the door right now." I kissed my son on his forehead as he was beginning to drift off to sleep, and I waved to my mother. I left out the door, praying tonight would not be the night that my car acted up by not starting.

Throughout my entire life, I didn't think any man had ever made me feel the way Eric did. He paid attention to me all night, stayed by my side, and introduced me to all of his coworkers. Everyone was so friendly and made me feel as though I belonged and fit in.

"You enjoying yourself?" Eric asked, his lips pressed against my ear, his warm breath gently gliding across my skin. He smelled like Hennessy and the fragrance Cool Water; it was fucking exotic if you asked me. His hand rested on my lower back as he leaned into me.

I looked at him and smiled. "Yes, everyone is really nice." As I spoke, Eric's eyes were glued to my lips, and he flicked the tip of his tongue over his upper lip.

Shit! I wanted to jump this man. I mean I wanted to lay him down and do everything sexually possible that one could do to another human being.

"Did I tell you how beautiful you look tonight?" He did actually. He told me when he first laid eyes on me, and he told me two other times after that.

"Um, I think you did, yeah." We chuckled as he dipped his head so that he could plant a kiss on my cheek.

"What time do you have to get back to your mom's house?"

We stared at each other as my breath caught in my throat. "Midnight," I said softly as he began rubbing my lower back.

"Like Cinderella?" He snickered. We were so close to each other that I felt his body warmth. "Can I have you for myself before you get back home?"

Jesus! My pussy was doing backflips in my boy shorts.

"OK," was the only word I was able to say. Eric took my hand and entwined our fingers and put them to his lips so he could kiss them. This man was sensual. He probably took his time when he had sex and made sure he treated the pussy with tender loving care. I myself preferred a little rough-neck loving, but for Eric, I didn't mind switching it up.

With our hands still interlocked, Eric and I said goodbye to his coworkers before we made our way to the parking lot.

"Follow me, alright, and try to keep up; I got a little bit of Vin Diesel in me." He laughed as he opened my car door, and I got in. Eric drove a Subaru, and he told no lies about his fast driving. I lost his ass twice as I followed him to his house. He had to pull over on the side of the road and wait for me.

"I told you to keep up." He laughed as he opened the door for me to climb out. Eric lived in a more upscale part of town, and his neighborhood was very quiet. His home was average sized. Inside, it was very masculine. You could tell it was a bachelor's pad—dark colors and leather everywhere.

I felt a bit nervous because truth be told, I had never once cheated on Khalil before. Even though he deserved it, I just never had it in me to be unfaithful.

"Why you look nervous? I don't bite… unless you want me to." Eric sat on a black leather sectional, pulling at his bottom lip with his fingers as he stared at me with his piercing, light-brown eyes. My feet were planted at the entrance of his front door as if I were contemplating making a run for it.

"Look, Jamika, if you don't wish to be here, it's cool. I understand your situation."

I looked over at him, and I'd never wanted a man so much in my life. I devoured him with my eyes. His black Versace slacks hugged his toned thighs, and his long-sleeved sweater showed all the definitions of his upper body. Realizing I needed to stop acting like a pussy, I waltzed over to where he sat and plopped down loudly next to him.

"I'm straight." I looked at him and managed a weak smile.

"You sure?" I nodded my head, and he used that opportunity to grab my hand. He pulled me up from out of the seat.

"Come on, let me show you around my humble home."

We walked around as he showed me room after room. His house had two bedrooms with a bathroom in each one. He converted a third bedroom into a theatre room. The chairs in that room were so spacious; three people could fit in one of the chairs easily. We decided to stay in that room and watch a movie.

"What would you like to watch?" He handed me a collection of DVDs. As I flipped through them, Eric stood up and pulled his sweater over his head. I was left to gawk at his chiseled chest and abs, but something caught my eyes, though—something he had just above his left nipple. A very familiar tattoo was engraved in his chest. He saw me looking at it and smiled as he sat down next me.

"Everybody has a past, right?" he said as his fingers traced the letters on his tattoo.

"You-you were in a gang?"

He tugged at his bottom lips with his fingers again and ran the palm of his hands through his bald head. "Yup, I was a few years ago."

What! I screamed in my head. Eric, whom I never heard cuss not one time, was in a gang. What in the world? Talk about a curveball.

"And what happened?" I couldn't take my eyes off the letters on his chest.

"I was in a gang with my brother. We had the city locked. No one, and I do mean no one, dared to cross us. The weight we were moving was ridiculous, but you know, money brings enemies and fake friends—a lot of fake friends. Long story short, somebody from inside our camp tried to set me up when I went to make a drop, and I took a bullet straight to my chest. The doctors said it missed my heart by this close…" He put his index and middle finger up, showing how close he came to death. "I was in the hospital for almost a month. When I got out, I changed my life. I got out the game."

I mean, I heard what he said and all, but those words just weren't registering. The last thing I would have thought was that Eric was a dope boy. This shit was bananas.

"What about your brother? Where is he?" I questioned as he took my hand and began caressing my fingers.

"Oh, he's still doing his thing. The streets is his, and we don't speak much. He wasn't really feeling my decision to come out the game, but I did what I felt was right for me. He handled the guys that shot me. Every last one of them got a bullet between their eyes. I wasn't ready to die just yet, so I left the streets for him." He brought my fingers to his lips and began kissing the tips.

"What's your brother's name?" I was curious as fuck to know. I was originally from the hood, and I knew a few of the local dope boys, so I was pretty sure I knew Eric's brother. The only person I knew that had a lot of weight in the streets was Julissa's man, Shaun, but he didn't have a brother.

"I don't really feel like discussing my brother right now," Eric said as he looked down at his crotch. Following his gaze, I saw that his dick was rock hard, and I blushed at him.

"Why don't you stand right here and take that off." Eric pointed to the floor in front of him. I nervously stood up so that I could stand directly facing him. Eric leaned back in his seat and placed one hand on his bulge, while the other hand pulled on his lower lip. His eyes were filled with lust as he hungrily looked at me.

I reached for the straps of my romper but stopped. Eric wouldn't like my body. I mean, yeah, I lost some weight, but he wouldn't appreciate the stretchmarks on my stomach from a child I gave birth to that wasn't even his! He wouldn't appreciate my extra thick thighs that had a little cellulite. This was crazy.

"I don't have a body like those women in the rap videos," I said shyly as I looked down at my feet.

"Hey, look at me, Jamika."

I looked up at him, and he leaned forward so he could take my hand.

"Don't ever let anybody tell you, you're not beautiful. I don't care about those women in the rap videos; half of them are plastic anyway. I appreciate everything about you. I don't care if you have stretchmarks, or your stomach isn't as flat as it used to be. I don't care 'bout none of that. Don't feel embarrassed when you're in my presence... ever, aight?"

Jesus, this nigga right here! Nobody had ever said anything like that to me. I swore I felt like crying tears of joy.

I looked down at him and nodded my head in agreement. He leaned back in his seat once more and smiled at me.

"Good, now take your clothes off for me."

My confidence was now on a full hundred, and I pulled my romper down until it reached to my waist. I stepped out of my wedge heels so that I could take the romper completely off. I stood before Eric in my boy shorts and a strapless bra, and his eyes roamed over my curves slowly then traveled back to my eyes.

"Fuck, Jamika."

Did he just curse? I couldn't help but smile. "Oh my God, I've never heard you curse before, Eric."

"Oh, I may not be hood in the streets, but I'm definitely hood in the sheets."

Jesus, I think I'm in love with this man! Like for real, I'm gonna have to marry this nigga.

Reaching for my ass, he pulled me to him, and he began placing kisses on my stomach. He was kissing my stretchmarks, y'all! I looked down at him in awe and rubbed gently on his bald head. Taking his fingers, he hooked them in my boy shorts and tugged them down slowly until they fell on the floor around my ankles.

He kissed my thighs and bit into them gently, and a soft moan escaped my lips. Eric stood up and directed me to sit down. I sat at the edge of the seat, and he got on his knees between my thighs. With his hands on my knees, he parted my legs and wasted no time diving in.

Eric's tongue touched every spot. He licked, he sucked, and he had me saying his name over and over. He rotated his tongue against my clit, and I felt my orgasm close, so I grabbed his head by his ears, forcing him to stay in place. I grinded my pussy onto his greedy mouth as I was about to explode.

"Buss in my mouth, baby," Eric said against my pussy, and I lost it. My body convulsed as Eric groaned, lapping up the last of my juices. He reached up and kissed me, and I took his tongue in my mouth and sucked on it, tasting myself.

"Stand up," I instructed him. I reached for his pants and unzipped them. I took them off and eagerly freed his dick from his boxers. Eric's dick was long and thick with a pink tip. It even had a little curve to it.

I took his tip in my mouth and sucked as he groaned loudly and tilted his head back. I filled my mouth with the rest of his length as saliva ran out from my mouth as I expertly deepthroated his dick.

"Fuck, Jamika!" He held my face so that he could fuck my mouth with his dick, and I enjoyed the way he groaned and cursed under his breath. He pulled me away suddenly and took my hand, pulling me into a standing position. He turned me around, and I held on to the headrest of the seat. Eric put on a condom and positioned his head at my opening. I closed my eyes as he eased himself inside of me.

Eric started off slow at first with nice, long, deep strokes. With his hands on my shoulders, he guided his dick in and out of me.

"Fuck this pussy, baby," I said as I looked back at him. That was all he wanted to hear apparently. Slapping me hard on my ass, Eric pounded into me with no mercy. He was doing damage to my womb, my bladder… my motherfuckin' throat! His dick was hitting all my internal organs, I kid you not.

Forget what I said earlier. There was nothing gentle about Eric's sex. He told no lies about being hood in the sheets.

Roughly an hour after, I left Eric's house aching and sore but with a smile on my face. I reached for my cellphone in my glove compartment and saw I had a bunch of missed calls. My mother and Khalil were blowing up my phone.

"Shit," I said as I called my mom. She picked up after the first ring.

"You really have some nerve, Jamika," my mom said, sounding half asleep.

"I'm sorry. I'm on my way to get him now."

"Don't bring your ass over here! It's after one in the god damn morning! Come get him tomorrow, and yo' nigga kept calling for you! Tell that fool to lose my number!" she shouted at me before hanging up her phone. I tossed the phone on my lap as I made my way home. Since Khalil was obviously looking for me, I knew he was gonna be ready for a fight as soon as I walked through the door.

Thank God Eric had some bomb ass dick that was worth it because it was about to be World War III in a minute.

CHAPTER NINETEEN

Trent

"Nah, I'm good on that pussy." I roughly shoved LaLa out my way as I got ready to make my way on stage. The bitch had been in my face these last couple days, tryna jump on my dick. But we all knew by now, that pussy whack as hell.

I was busy oiling up my chest and abdominals while LaLa kept shouting in my ear.

"Bruh, why are you even in here? This is the men's locker room, so take your ass on somewhere." I stopped applying baby oil so that I could get all in her face because she was beginning to piss me off.

"Fuck you, Trent! Your dick game was weak any damn way!"

I snorted at her. I wasn't even worried about the shit coming out her bitter mouth.

"Tracey strokes my pussy better with her strap, nigga."

"Bitch, yo' pussy got invisible fuckin' walls! The fuck is you talking about? Now get the fuck on out my face before I drop you on your ass." I clenched my teeth as I mean mugged the hell out of her.

"That nerdy glasses face bitch sure do have you feeling yourself."

Not even giving it another thought, I reached for her throat and squeezed the fuck out of it. "Don't ever, in your motherfuckin' life, refer to her like that again. Put some respect on her name. And that nerd—as you call her—her pussy got mad grip, rather than that big cave pussy between yo' legs." I finished my sentence by pushing her to the ground.

"Damn, 'Dingo, you ain't gotta do shorty like that," another stripper named Magnum said as he walked in the same time I was handling LaLa, but he didn't even bother to help her off the floor either.

He looked down as he stepped over her to make his way to the locker.

"I told you, you should have given me the pussy, LaLa... Now look at you, sprawled out on the floor and shit," Magnum said as he began changing his clothes, as he'd just gotten off the stage.

Standing from off the floor, she dusted her ass off and began walking toward the door, and I turned away from her.

"Bruh, that pussy weak as fuck. You don't want them problems." Magnum and I laughed as he gave me daps. "Besides, her girlfriend, Tracey, is the one with the tight pum pum. We used to fuck like rabbits every chance we got." I continued laughing, not even bothering to make sure if LaLa had left the room completely.

"You used to fuck Tracey behind my back, Trent?" LaLa seethed at me as she came to stand in front my face once more.

"Man, you still in here? Get the fuck out my face before I drop you on your shit again!" I shouted at her as I pointed at the door.

She looked me dead in my eyes and gave me a cold, hard, evil stare. "You'll live to regret the day you fucked me over," she said icily as she spun on her heels to walk out the door.

"Ain't nobody worried 'bout you, LaLa." I waved her off as I closed the cap of my baby oil bottle.

"Niggaaaaa, you got that cocaine dick! Bitch going through withdrawal symptoms," Magnum cracked, and I busted out laughing as the DJ announced my name to go on stage.

I left the locker room and made my way on stage. The crowd was hype as I walked slowly out on stage. The thirst traps, as usual, made their way to the front of the stage, waving their bills at me.

Standing at the center of the stage, I allowed my hand to slowly run down my chest and then to my abs as I held the gaze of a few women. It was important to make each and every one of these ladies feel as though I was dancing just for them. It made them feel as though I was in love with them, like I wanted to put this big motherfucker up in their guts, but truly, my mind was on Destiny. I had to admit to myself that I was really feeling Destiny, and after she spent the night at my house, it was a wrap.

We were definitely feeling the hell out of each other, and when she finally told me she called it off with that lame ass nigga that she was involved with, that shit was just icing on the cake. Finally, I had her all to myself. I actually planned to visit her after I left the club. I couldn't get enough of her fine ass.

"'Dingoooooo! Come here, zaddy!" an oversized woman screamed out at me. I knew her well, and she always shoved only hundreds in my drawers. I gyrated my hips as I made my way over to where she was at the edge of the stage.

She wasted no time caressing my legs as her hand inched up my thigh. Placing my hand over hers, I guided her to my dick and showed her how I wanted her to play with my monster. Her eyes bulged in her head when she felt what I was working with. I winked at her as our eyes locked, and she quickly shoved about four hundred dollars in the waistband of my loin cloth.

My attention went to the bar, and LaLa and Tracey were involved in a heated argument, which ended in LaLa slapping the taste out of Tracey before she stormed out.

My dick had gotten me into trouble countless of times, so I really wasn't worried about the lover's quarrel with those two. My eyes focused on a figure that was making her way to the stage. She was sexy as hell. She wore a fitted, short leather dress, her thick thighs on full display. One of her thighs had a tattoo of a peacock with the tail all the way down to her knee. She was slightly bowlegged as she walked, and that's when I realized that walk looked awfully familiar.

My eyes traveled up to her face, and I froze in shock. It was Clarissa. She came to stand at the edge of the stage, a handful of money in her grasp. I smiled at her like we were teenagers again, about to thief a fuck in my parents' home. I bent so I could get closer to her.

"I always knew that big dick would be famous one day," she said as she shoved her money in my waist.

****

"I hadn't planned on staying, but I've been back like two months now." Clarissa and I sat outside the club in my car, catching up on old times. She told me she came back to town because her mother died. It had been a minute since I was back in my old neighborhood, so I had no idea.

"Tricia did mention that she saw you. Was she the one that told you I worked here?" I looked at her and couldn't believe how fine she looked. Even with the slight age difference between us, she didn't look older than me at all.

"Nah, this was just a big coincidence. I came here by myself actually. I just wanted to see what inside a male strip club was like. Imagine my surprise when I saw you doing your thing on stage." She pushed my arm as she laughed, showing perfect white, even teeth.

"It's just temporary, though." I shrugged my shoulders as I began rubbing my beard. I should've been on my way over to Destiny's house, but I'd leave as soon as Clarissa and I were done catching up.

"The ladies sure seem to love you." She looked me over as she licked her lips. Shit! My dick reacted to her instantly. After all these years, Clarissa could still make my dick rock up by just giving me that look.

"Anyway, I better be going. I have to call an Uber to come get me," she said as she reached for the handle of door. I knew I shouldn't have, but a nigga felt like he had the devil on one shoulder and an angel on the other, both giving different advice.

"I can drop you off. Where you staying at?"

****

Bang! Bang! Bang!

The headboard of Clarissa's bed knocked against the wall as I fucked the shit out of her. Don't even ask a nigga how he ended up in this motherfuckin' position with Clarissa's legs on top of my shoulders. All I remembered was her directing me to an apartment where she'd been staying since she came to town. She asked me if I wanted to come inside to look around, and the next thing I knew, she had my dick so far down her throat that I was seeing stars.

"Yeah, rub on that clit while I beat this pussy up," I instructed her. Placing her fingers between her thighs, she made circular motions on her juicy clit as she licked her lips over and over again, never taking her eyes off me.

"Ssssss, fuck, Trent. You got even better at this." She moaned as I continued to pound in and out of her. Looking down between us, I could see my condom-covered dick going in and out of her wet pussy. I reached up, grabbed her throat, and applied a little pressure.

Oh, Clarissa still liked this rough shit. I felt her walls begin to tighten as her eyes rolled to the back of her head. She was about to bust, and I was cumming right along with her.

"Mmmmm… Aaaaah… Fuckkkkk!" I was sounding like a bitch as I exploded inside the condom.

"Shit, Trent!" Clarissa screamed as she clawed at my back. I collapsed on top of her as I fought to catch my breath.

Five minutes later, I was seeing about my hygiene when my phone began ringing again inside my pants pocket that laid on the ground, for like the tenth time. I already knew it was Destiny calling.

"You got a girl?" Clarissa asked as she sat naked, Indian style in the bed as she rolled up a blunt. I shook my head because old habits die hard. She did that when we were younger also.

Picking my pants up from off the floor, I dressed quickly, preparing to leave from somewhere I should have never ended up in the first place. But it was a little too late for that.

"Yeah, something like that," I said as I grabbed my car keys from her night table and headed to the door.

CHAPTER TWENTY

Destiny

"Stay still, Jamika, damn!" I fussed at my friend as I rubbed the antibiotic cream on the bruises to her face. She spent the night at my house after Khalil beat her ass for coming home late on Friday night. She called me to come and get her at about two in the damn morning.

"Just leave it, Destiny. I'll see about it myself as soon as I get up," she snapped at me for like the second time since I got here.

"I'm just trying to help your ass." I put the ointment down and took a seat in a chair next to the bed. She sighed loudly and closed her eyes for a couple seconds before she opened them to look at me.

"I'm sorry, Destiny. I know you're just trying to help." Jamika had a black and blue eye, a few scratches on her face, and a couple of bruised ribs. She said when she got home from being out with Eric, Khalil was waiting for her ass as soon as she walked through the door. He asked where she was all night, and before she even got a chance to reply, he dealt a blow straight to her face. After he was done beating on her, he told her she wasn't allowed to go to the gym again. He threw her cell phone against the wall and stormed out their apartment.

"He was so mad, Destiny, I thought he was about to kill me for real," she said softly as her eyes filled with tears. I grabbed ahold of her hand and squeezed gently.

"Khalil had a lot of nerve. He has done more dirt to you than I care to remember. The last thing he should be doing is putting his hands on you." I was mad as hell, but I was trying not to show it. I wished I was a man; I would have found Khalil and beat his ass myself.

"I'll just stay out of the gym for now." My mouth popped open at what she said because I saw that she was enjoying working out. She was more confident, she was smiling more, and now she was going to let that punk Khalil ruin it for her.

"Jamika, girl, don't do that. Don't let him win. Look how much you've accomplished in such a short time, and Eric motivated you. What has Khalil ever done to push you to be great? All that nigga ever does is complain. Don't let him push you over." I tried my best to be a one-woman cheer squad for my girl, but she just shook her head.

"Look at me. Who was I tryna fool? I need to accept the fact that this is how and who I am. A fat baby momma that nobody wants." Silent sobs escaped her as she put her face into the palm of her hands. My heart broke for Jamika because she always did this. She always underestimated herself and her beauty.

"Jamika, I done told you so many times how beautiful you are. Don't let Khalil get in your head. Didn't you say how good that nigga Eric made you feel? Girl, get that man and make that nigga yours. Fuck Khalil." Yeah, I said it! I didn't like his ass any damn way.

Jamika managed a weak smile. "You turned gangster on me all of a sudden," she said as she wiped her eyes, and I reached in to hug her.

"You damn right. You my girl, and I got your back."

She snickered at me and hugged me back. "Speaking about gangster, you would never believe this." We pulled away from each other, and I waited for her to continue talking.

"Eric was part of a gang. I saw his tattoo on his chest." I was shocked at what she said since her description of Eric was so clean cut.

"A gang? Didn't you say he never curses or anything."

"Yup, turns out his brother and him use to run the streets. But Eric got shot and almost died, so he left the game. His brother sounds like he's still in pretty deep, though." I listened attentively to her and didn't make much of what she said. I didn't know as much about the local dope boys as Jamika did, so I couldn't really shed any light on the conversation.

"Well, at least he's out the game now. You wanna use my phone to give him a call since Khalil broke yours?"

"Not right now. Maybe later, though. Can I use it to call Julissa? I want her to go over to my house so she can get me a change of clothes and stuff."

I sucked my teeth so loud that shit echoed through the room. "I don't want that bitch over at my house, Jamika." I curled my lips in disgust.

"Can you chill with the petty shit? I just want her to get some of my stuff. I'm not about to go back over there just yet, and I know you don't want to go just in case you run into Khalil." I was actually contemplating not lending her my phone. Huffing softly, I shoved the phone at her, and she took it from me.

I listened as she spoke to Julissa and gave her directions to my home so that she could come get Jamika's house keys. My mind drifted off to Trent as I waited for her to get off the phone.

I called Trent repeatedly last night, but he didn't pick up his phone. He was supposed to come over after working his shift at the club last night. But I was calling to let him know that Jamika was here, and we had to take a rain check; however, he never answered any of my calls.

He did send me a message back a couple hours after, saying his shift ended late and that it was cool that I was looking out for my friend, and we would meet up soon. He never tried to contact me today, though, which was a bit odd, but I figured he was just giving me time alone with Jamika.

"She's on her way over." I rolled my eyes as I took my cellphone from her hand. "Can you chill and be on your best behavior, damn!" Jamika chuckled, but I just sucked my teeth at her. Julissa was her friend... not mine!

Half an hour later, Julissa showed up. I had planned to walk out to give her Jamika's keys, but this bitch was knocking at my door before I even got there.

I took a deep breath before I turned the knob.

"Hey, girl, where's Jamika at?" This rude heffa just pushed through my door and walked in my house! We were not good like that.

"Excuse you, Julissa. You could have at least waited for me invite your ass inside." I looked at her as she turned to me, looking me up and down as if I were the one who intruded into her home.

"Girl, we all family. It's cool." I should drop this bitch right where she stood. Talking 'bout family. I decided to hurry on up and let Jamika deal with her fake ass friend so that she could hurry and get the hell out my house.

"Jamika!" I shouted out to her. "Julissa's here! You want me come get the keys for her?"

Jamika shouted out to me that she would come down and give them to her. Julissa eyed me from the tips of my toes to the top of my head as if she were trying to figure something out about me. She gave me a fake ass smile before she sat down on my sofa.

She wore a barely-there denim skirt that exposed her tattoo-covered thighs with a thin strapped top and a pair of low-cut Converse on her feet.

"Hey, Julissa." Jamika took her time and walked to where Julissa sat, holding on to her side.

Julissa's eyebrows lifted as she gawked at Jamika's appearance. "Damn, Jamika! Did you at least pinch the nigga? He fucked you up!"

My blood grew hot. Instead of this trick trying to at least be sympathetic toward her friend, she sounded as if she was cracking on her.

"Girl, shut up and go get my stuff. I need to leave Destiny's place by tonight. She's probably tired of seeing me," Jamika said as she handed Julissa her house keys.

"You could stay as long as you want, boo." I smiled warmly at her. I could have sworn Julissa rolled her eyes at us.

"I know you want your privacy for when Trent comes over. It's cool, girl." I rolled my eyes 'cause I didn't know why she had my business running out her mouth to this stank bitch. Julissa got this funny look on her face at the mention of Trent's name. She ran her eyes over me as if she were somehow mad.

"Trent? Which Trent is that?" Her nostrils flared in and out as she waited for a reply. Jamika, with her big mouth, went right ahead and cleared up Julissa's confusion.

"Girl, that fine ass stripper that rescued us from the club a few weeks ago."

I started getting a weird vibe like nothing good was about to come from this conversation, so I decided to try and change the subject.

"Anyway, Julissa probably wants to get going," I said, making my way to the front door so this bitch could hurry up and leave.

"You mean 'Dingo!" she all but shouted out Trent's stage name. She stood up and had a smirk on her face.

"Girl, don't get caught up with that nigga. We fucked the other night." The room got so quiet that I swore I heard all of our hearts beating at different intervals. Jamika's jaw dropped as she turned to me, her eyes wide.

I was trying really hard not to lose it. Before I went ahead and believed what this trick was saying, I decided to play it cool.

Julissa was now standing in my face, and I narrowed my eyes at her in anger… but I stayed quiet.

"I didn't know you guys were a couple. When he invited me over at his house, I would have sworn he was single. Niggas ain't shit, girl." She smiled at me as I let her words sink in. So Trent invited Julissa, whom by the way, he called a hoe, over to his place. Trent practically begged me to leave Miguel, and all for what? So that he could play me?

"Girl, I ain't trippin'. Go ahead and have that nigga. Please raise on up out my house, though." I wasn't about to stand here and fight over a nigga that wasn't mine to begin with. Jamika came and stood next to us. She was looking worried as if something was about to jump off.

"Julissa, you ain't right. You got a nigga. You lucky he never found out about your cheating ass."

Julissa snorted and waved Jamika off. "Casper is too busy in the streets to even know what I'm doing. He don't care. Let me go ahead and run over to your house. Khalil won't be there, right?"

"I can't say for certain, but if he is, just ignore his ass and bring me my stuff."

Jamika was a whole fool for trusting Julissa, in any shape or form… I swore. As Julissa began walking in the direction of my front door, she just couldn't help herself, so she stopped and looked at me.

"My bad about 'Dingo, Destiny. Now that I know y'all are involved, I'll stop riding that big motherfucker he got between his legs." It took everything… and I do mean everything, in me not to headbutt her ass. She sashayed her ass out my door and made her way to her car.

I slammed my front door so hard that I was surprised it didn't fly off the hinges.

"Destiny—" Before Jamika could even form her sentence, I held my hand up at her for her to be quiet.

"Save it, Jamika. It's only because I respect myself way too much. That's the only reason I didn't stab that bitch. You trust her? To go over to your place with Khalil being there?" I chuckled under my breath. "You can't trust that bitch around a dog in heat, but you'll trust her to be around your man?"

Jamika looked at me as if I had gone insane. "Nah, Destiny, I told you many times Khalil can't stand Julissa, and vice versa. Just because Trent can't keep his dick in his pants doesn't mean my man would fuck a hoe like Julissa."

I felt like Jamika slapped me across my face with her words. She realized what she said and immediately tried to apologize.

"You know what? It's cool. I mean, it's my own fault, right? I was stupid enough to fall for a man that strips for women. It's my own fault for trying to be a good friend and look out for you and warn you about Julissa. It's my own fault for not minding my business by letting you know Julissa ain't really your friend. So going forward, I'll just go on ahead and mind my own motherfucking business."

Making my way across to where my keys for my ride were, I picked them up.

"Destiny, I didn't mean it like that. Where are you going?" Jamika asked as I made my way hastily out the front door.

"Be sure when I get back… you're not here." My hands were shaking as I walked to my car. Jamika called out to me a couple of times, but I ignored her ass. I unlocked my door as I jumped into the driver's seat. Putting the key into the ignition, I burned rubber as I pulled out and sped down my street.

I swore I had nothing but murder on my mind as I made my way to Trent's home.

CHAPTER TWENTY-ONE

Jamika

"Destiny!" I called out to her as she power walked to her car. Why did I have to open my big mouth and say something so stupid to the one person who I knew for a fact cared so much about me? I stood and watched as she drove off down the street. I was certain she was going to see Trent. I only prayed she didn't get a murder charge when she was done dealing with his ass.

Julissa was foul as hell for that little stunt she just pulled. She could have just let that piece of information about her and Trent fucking slide, but she just had to go and open her big mouth. Sometimes, I felt Destiny might've been right about her. Sometimes, I felt she wasn't as true a friend as she said she was.

I slowly made my way to the bedroom Destiny allowed me to sleep in so that I could go and collect my belongings. Khalil sure did a number on me when I got home. I was sore all over, and my sides hurt like hell from where he kicked me. My eye was swollen from where he punched me, and I had a busted lip.

When I walked into our house, he was sitting up in the living room in the dark, waiting for my ass. I was hoping he wouldn't have been home, but by the amount of missed calls I had from him when I left Eric's house, I knew I was about to get it.

"Where you now coming from, Jamika?" His voice almost caused me to have a heart attack as I tiptoed through the living room.

"I-I to-told you, remember, that I was going to be over at my mother's."

See, this was why I never cheated before. My dumb ass couldn't even tell a lie without stuttering. Khalil got up from where he sat and slithered to where I stood. He slowly drank me in, from my wedge shoes to my outfit to the light make up on my face. I stood so still that I forget I needed to breathe.

When I tell y'all... I did not see that slap coming until my head almost spun around like that chick from the exorcist... Khalil slapped me like a hooker that came up short on her pimp's money.

"You must think I'm stupid," he spat at me as I reached for my stinging cheek. Tears burned my eyes just as much as that slap burned my face.

"Bitch, what kind of book club is it where u needed to dress like that? Huh? Makeup on your face, that tight ass suit on. You think you all that because you lost a little weight? You thought you could start cheating on me with some no-good nigga! Bitch, I'll kill you and him!"

Before I could respond or even move away from him, he grabbed me by my hair and tossed me to the floor. I counted a total of seven kicks I got from his Air Force sneakers.

"Let me hear you've been back at that gym, I'mma dead yo' stupid ass."

I was balled up in the fetal position, and pain racked my body as I fought to breathe. My ribs felt like they were bruised. Khalil searched for my phone from my clutch purse and stomped on it before leaving out the house.

I literally crawled to where we had our house phone and called Destiny up to come and get me.

I changed from the pajama bottoms and top Destiny gave me to sleep in and put my own belongings on, deciding I should just leave Destiny's house. Making sure I took everything, I walked over to the house phone and dialed Julissa to let her know I wouldn't need her to get my stuff after all. I was just going to go home, pack a few of my clothes, and head over to my mother's house so that I could be with my son.

I called Julissa about three times, but she never picked up. I knew she should have been at my place by now since Destiny and I didn't live that far away from each other.

Not even bothering to try calling Julissa a fourth time, I called an Uber to come get me to take me over to my house.

On my drive home, thoughts of Eric invaded my mind, and even though I was banged up pretty good, I actually couldn't lie. Eric's sex was worth the pain my ass was in at the moment. I had no idea how we would be able to see each other again. Whoever was spying on me at the gym was doing a damn good job. Khalil knew my every move. Even if I wanted to go back to the gym to see Eric again, I couldn't go until I was healed.

We pulled up to my apartment, and I thanked the driver and got out. I was hoping Julissa was still here so she wouldn't have wasted her time to go all the way back over to Destiny's place. I turned the knob and pushed the door open, I was really hoping Khalil wasn't here so I could just be in and out as fast as I could.

As I walked toward our bedroom, I began hearing what sounded like voices. I stopped and waited with my head tilted to the side to see if I was hearing things. But the voice came again, a little louder this time, and it sounded like Julissa.

Why did she sound as if she was moaning, though? With cat-like steps, I creeped up to the bedroom door that was slightly open.

"Suck on that clit, baby."

I held on to my bruised ribs as hot tears flowed from my eyes. My man, the father of my son, the man I had been with since high school, was on his knees, between the legs of somebody that was supposed to be my friend, munching on her pussy as she sat on *our* bed. The bed that I laid my head on and the bed that we had sex in countless of times, that exact same bed.

"This pussy fucking juicy, mmmmm." Khalil moaned as he smacked his lips against Julissa's pussy lips.

"Is it better than Jamika's? Say it… Tell me it's better than hers as you eat me out," Julissa said as she placed her hand on the top of his head and grinded her slit in my man's face. I knew he was about to say it, so I didn't wait for the words to pass his lips. I turned and made my way out of the house.

I stumbled out into the street, walking aimlessly with no location in mind. I was heartbroken. How could I be so fucking stupid? How could I have been so fucking trusting? Destiny tried to warn me so many times. I wondered how long they'd been fucking each other behind my back.

My tears blinded my vision as I walked along the street, and what I saw clouded my train of thought, so much so that I didn't see the car coming toward me as I attempted to cross the street... until it was too late.

I was thrown into the air, and when I fell to the ground, my head hit the concrete on the sidewalk hard. A few seconds after, everything went black.

CHAPTER TWENTY-TWO

Trent

I swore I fucked so much pussy in my life that most of them, I couldn't even remember the women's names. But I'd never fucked a bitch and felt as bad about doing it as I felt right now.

I couldn't even bring myself to call Destiny today. I stayed in my room all day and didn't even bother showing up for work at the auto shop either.

It was like Clarissa was the devil, I swore, and she came back into my life just to prove I was a ain't shit nigga. And I most definitely was. I didn't even think twice about dropping her panties. It was like I had a better understanding of what women meant when they said the man who took their virginity would always have a special place in their heart.

That was how I felt when I saw Clarissa again. It seemed as if all my feelings from when I was younger resurfaced again. Did I wish to pursue something with Clarissa again? No, I didn't. However, I wanted to see what that pussy did, and I did; it was great… but I didn't plan to

175

do it again.

I felt like I somehow betrayed Destiny. I mean, I caused all sorts of problems to make sure she left her nigga, just so I could have her all to myself. Then after I did that, I went and fucked somebody that I had no right fucking from ever since I was a kid.

The word on the street was the reason Clarissa left when she was eighteen to live with her boyfriend was that her father started molesting her when she was just about thirteen years old, and that was really the reason behind her leaving. At first, I didn't want to believe those stories, but then when I got older, I thought it kind of made sense. Maybe that was why she targeted me at that age—because she was doing what she knew. This was the same thing with Tricia being with niggas who beat her ass. They became a product of their environment.

Realizing that I was in bed longer than I should have been, I got up and put a pair of boxers on. It was eerily quiet at my home, which was something odd because Heaven usually came jumping on my bed in the morning to wake me up. I opened my door and made my way into my living room, and it was empty. Rubbing my hands through my fade, I walked into the kitchen and decided that Heaven and Tricia were probably sleeping late. I started making a cup of coffee, my mind wandering back to Clarissa, and I hoped I didn't run into her again any time soon.

As I was about to go knock on Tricia's bedroom door, I heard my cellphone ringing in my room. I turned around, made my way inside, and picked the phone off the bed. It was my coworker from the club Magnum. What the fuck did he want? We weren't really that cool for this nigga to be calling my phone first thing in the morning.

"Yoooo?" I said as I answered, walking back out of my room.

"Bruh, you will never believe this shit."

I stopped at the front of Tricia's door because the sound of his voice made my movements pause. He sounded hyped.

"What's the deal? What happened?"

"Tracey's dead!"

I paused midway from knocking on Tricia's door, confused by what he just said.

"Who Tracey?" I asked. My eyebrows knitted together as I waited for confirmation.

"Nigga, Tracey, Tracey, LaLa's girlfriend."

What the hell? I rubbed my hand in my hair, not knowing what else to do.

"What the fuck? How did it happen, and who told you?" I knocked softly on Tricia's bedroom door.

"LaLa called me, bawling her eyes out a short while ago. She said she went out to have a few drinks after she left the club with some friends, and Tracey went home alone. When she got back home, Tracey was already dead on the kitchen floor with a knife to her chest. Police believe it may have been a robbery gone bad."

I shook my head in disbelief because that shit was crazy. Tracey was good people and didn't need to be killed like that. Realizing Tricia wasn't opening the door, I opened it my damn self.

"Fuck," I cursed out loud as I glared inside the empty room.

"You good, man?" Magnum asked after my sudden outburst.

"Let me call you right back." Not even giving him time to reply, I hung up the phone. I walked around the empty room and stood by the bed. It looked as if no one had slept in it the night before. When I got home from by Clarissa's, it was late, so I assumed Tricia and Heaven were already asleep. From the looks of things, she wasn't even here when I got home. I knew damn well Tricia did not go back to that nigga's apartment, taking my niece with her. I would beat her ass myself.

Rage took over my emotions because I knew that's exactly what she did. I dialed her number, but it went straight to voicemail.

Walking to my room, I began getting dressed, saying every curse word I knew. When I pulled up to that nigga's place, everybody better run for cover, I felt the old Trent surfacing—the Trent that turned into Hulk when provoked. What the fuck was wrong with my sister, putting my niece through that type torment of seeing her mother get pounded on by a disrespectful ass nigga?

As I was done lacing up my Timberland boots because I was prepared to kick somebody's teeth out, my phone rang again. Grabbing it, I didn't even check the caller ID before I answered.

"Tricia! Where the fuck did you take my ni—"

"Hello? Is this Trent Bishop?" I quickly moved the phone from my ear to check the screen, only then realizing the number was an unfamiliar one.

"Who the fuck is this?"

"Sir, we're going to need to you to come down to the hospital. There has been an incident." My heart started racing like a motherfucker. My chest tightened, and I wondered if I was having a heart attack.

"An incident? What type of incident? Yo, who is this? Where's my niece and sister?" The room started spinning as I waited for some type of response.

"This is the police. We were going through your sister's phone and found your number. You need to get to the hospital as soon as you can, sir. It's very urgent."

I was panicking. I raced around my room, looking for my car keys, and those motherfuckers were nowhere to be found. Where the fuck did I put them? "Can you tell me if my niece is OK?" Finally finding the keys that were right in front of my face the whole time, I ran out of my room to the front door.

"I cannot." My heart dropped to the floor.

"What you mean, you can't, man?" Shit, the only person that had my emotions all over the place was Heaven-Leigh. If something bad happened to her, I didn't think I could take it.

"Sir, I'm not allowed to give any more information over the phone. You need to get to the hospital." After he told me what hospital I needed to get to, I ended the call and pulled the front door open only to be greeted by a very angry Destiny.

I was about to let her know something bad happened to my sister and niece when she raised her hand and slapped me across my face.

Nah, y'all don't understand. Destiny picked the wrong motherfucking morning to be on this bullshit.

"You fucked Julissa, nigga!"

What the fuck type of morning was this? I thought to myself.

Narrowing my eyes at her in anger, I wrapped my hand around her throat, not even thinking about what I was doing.

The old Trent was back.

TO BE CONTINUED...

FOLLOW ME ON FACEBOOK:

Amanda Rosales

Text ROYALTY to 42828 to join our mailing list!

To submit a manuscript for our review, email us at
submissions@royaltypublishinghouse.com

Text RPHCHRISTIAN to 22828 for our
CHRISTIAN ROMANCE novels!

Text RPHROMANCE to 22828 for our
INTERRACIAL ROMANCE novels!

Get LiT!

Download the LiTeReader app today and enjoy exclusive

content, free books, and more

CPSIA information can be obtained
at www.ICGtesting.com
Printed in the USA
LVOW13s0326170518
577422LV00022B/346/P